Praise for Fredric Brown:

"The essence of Fredric Brown's work is uniqueness. He is one of the most ingenious writers of his time with a lucid style that cleverly disguises complex plot and original themes."

—*Crime and Mystery Writers*

MURDER
CAN BE
FUN

FREDRIC BROWN

Carroll & Graf Publishers, Inc.
New York

Copyright © 1948 by Fredric Brown
Copyright renewed 1976 by Fredric Brown
All rights reserved

First Carroll & Graf edition 1989

Published by arrangement with Roberta Pryor, Inc

Carroll & Graf Publishers, Inc.
260 Fifth Avenue
New York, NY 10001

ISBN: 0-88184-504-3

Manufactured in the United States of America

MURDER CAN BE FUN

CHAPTER 1

THERE ARE few streets in America down which a man wearing a mask can walk without attracting undue attention. Broadway, Manhattan, is one of those streets; Broadway has carried sophistication to the point of naïveté.

The man in the mask had stepped out of a car parked just around the corner from Broadway, on a street in the upper Fifties. Many people must have seen him leave the car, but it didn't matter. Even if the police, afterward, had traced him back to that car, it still wouldn't have mattered. It was a stolen car, and one whose theft would not be reported for several hours to come.

His bright red costume would not have been noticed at all in December. Now, under a sweltering August sun, it drew casually curious glances from some of the people he passed. A few went so far as to turn their heads after him and to wonder slightly why there wasn't an advertising placard on his back. Surely he must be advertising or selling *something*. No one in his right mind would wear a hot flannel Santa Claus suit in August unless he was advertising or selling *something*.

But even if the man in the Santa Claus suit and mask wasn't in his right mind, that didn't matter to the casually curious. They knew it was a gag of some sort, and only suckers get curious about things that don't concern them. Pretty soon he'd turn into a doorway and start spieling—and then it would turn out that he was selling Santa Claus soap, a quarter a bar, guaranteed to wash the skins off potatoes so you wouldn't need a knife to peel them.

But the man in the Santa suit didn't stop to spiel or to peel. He kept on walking, not rapidly, but with the businesslike stride of a man who knows where he is going.

As a disguise, it was perfect. The scarlet suit and the plump-cheeked, cheery false face gave the lie to his actual height and build so successfully that he would not have needed a pillow tied to his midriff to have induced many to swear that he was short and fat. Afterward, the police would locate a dozen or so of the thousands of people who had passed him, and their reports would be conflicting to the point of absurdity. To the orthodox among them, he'd been fat and dumpy. To a few, the agnostics, he was tall and would have been skinny except for the pillow. Or had it been a pillow?

Height: short or tall. Build: fat or thin. Color of eyes: not known. Distinguishing features: Are you kidding?

That was the sum total of description, then, that the police obtained, and they did not find it helpful to them. They did, however, trace his route from the upper Fifties to the lower Fifties. And, after the murder, back again to the upper Fifties. But we get ahead of ourselves.

The man in the Santa suit went into a building in the lower Fifties. An elevator whisked him to the third floor, and he walked along the corridor to an office and opened a door marked simply ARTHUR D. DINEEN.

There was a railing across the room just inside the door. Beyond the railing a stenographer sat at a typing desk. She looked up as the Santa suit entered, and her eyes widened a little.

"I have an appointment with Mr. Dineen," said the voice behind the mask.

"You—uh—" The eyes of the stenographer whisked from the clock on the wall to the memo pad on her desk and then to the smiling, apple-cheeked mask. She said, "Your name, please?" with the smug air of one who is not to be taken in.

"Johan Smith," said the man in the red suit. "Mr. Dineen is expecting me at ten-fifteen."

Yes, that was the name on the memo pad, and he couldn't have read it from where he stood outside the railing. The girl at the desk said, "Yes, Mr. Smith. You may go in."

He walked through the gate in the railing and toward the door marked PRIVATE leading to the inner office.

The girl's eyes followed him speculatively. A screwball? Well, it wasn't her worry if he was. The boss himself had made the appointment. She remembered now that it had been made by telephone the previous afternoon. An actor, of course, but why would he wear a costume to the interview unless he was a screwball?

The man in the red suit didn't look back. He walked through the door and closed it after him, quietly.

The man seated at the desk in the inner office looked up. He saw the costume and said, "What in hell—?"

At the tone of his voice, there was a growl from the far corner of the room. A big Doberman pinscher who had been curled up in the shaft of sunlight from the open window was now on his feet. There was an ominous buzz saw in his chest.

The eyes that looked out through the holes in the false face flickered from the growling dog back to the gray-haired man at the desk. The voice from within the mask said, "If you don't want that pooch killed, tell him—" He didn't waste words finishing the sentence; the pistol now in his hands was more eloquent than speech—it was silently eloquent, one might say, for there was a silencer on the pistol.

His eyes narrowing as he took in the fact of the silenced revolver, the man behind the desk kept his hands carefully quiet on the blotter pad. He asked, "What do you want?"

"I *don't* want trouble," said the man in the Santa suit. "So first order that dog to lie down. I didn't know he'd be—" He stopped talking with the suddenness of one who realizes he is saying something he shouldn't.

The Doberman had taken two stiff-legged steps forward, and the buzz saw was louder. At rest, he had been sleekly beautiful; now he was savagely, threateningly beautiful. His eyes were intent; the short hairs on his neck, around the heavy collar with the gold-plated studs, stood menacingly erect.

His legs bent under him, like springs, even as the man at the desk turned his head. He said "Rex!"—but too late. Or perhaps the dog misinterpreted the order. He sprang.

3

There was a muffled explosion—about as loud as a cap pistol—as the man in the red suit pulled the trigger of the gun. He stepped aside as the body of the dog completed its arc through the air and thudded to the thickly carpeted floor of the office, twitched once, and lay still.

The man at the desk had leaped to his feet, his face twisted with anger. He said "Damn you" and snatched at the only heavy object on the desk top, an exquisitely made silver inkstand, and jerked it back over his shoulder to hurl it at the man in the red suit. Also, he opened his mouth to yell for help.

But the second muffled shot of the silenced gun stopped both the throw and the yell. The gray-haired man fell forward across the desk, and there was a small hole in his forehead, just above the left eye. The silver inkstand was the center of a spreading black pool on the carpet beside the swivel chair.

With cool deliberation, the man in the Santa Claus suit pocketed the pistol he had fired twice. He said, rather loudly in case any sounds had been heard in the office outside, "Yes, Mr. Dineen, I quite appreciate that. But—" And he kept on talking while he walked around the desk and picked up the fallen inkstand.

He held it upside down a moment while the last drops of ink ran out, then snapped the lid down over the well, and wrapped it carefully in a cloth before he put it into his pocket.

Then, leisurely, he walked to the door and held it slightly ajar. He said, "Good-bye then, Mr. Dineen. Sorry you couldn't see the proposition my way but—well, maybe some other network will give the idea a break."

He slid his hands into the white cotton gloves which he had worn up to the moment he had entered the inner office, and on his way out he let his gloved hands rub the doorknobs on both sides of the door to obliterate any prints he might have left there.

He strode through the outer office, past the stenographer, without speaking, walking with the injured dignity of a man whose pet idea has just been stepped on.

4

Disdaining the elevator, he walked down two flights of stairs and out into the Broadway crowd. A child saw him and said, "Mama! Look, isn't that—?" and was shushed into silence.

His departure from the scene of the murder drew no more— and no less—attention than had his arrival.

*   *   *

The newspaper story of what the press called the Santa Claus Murder was interesting reading to the public in general. But no one else found it as *damnably* interesting as did Bill Tracy when he bought a late afternoon paper and read it in his two-room kitchenette apartment before he went out to dinner.

He read it twice rapidly and a third time very slowly, as though weighing each word and seeking a meaning hidden behind it. Finally he put down the paper and stared for a while at the chaste pattern of the wallpaper. After a while he said a word which should not be repeated here, then picked up the paper and read the story again.

It was still there and it hadn't changed a bit.

It came to Tracy then that the only logical thing to do was to go out and get drunk. Not mildly inebriated, as he often was, but good and stinkingly drunk. Disgustingly drunk.

Not merely because he knew Arthur Dineen, the murdered man, nor yet because he knew Rex, the almost-murdered Doberman, who had been creased by a bullet grooving his skull, but who would recover. Tracy had rather liked Dineen, and he had greatly liked Rex, even though he had seen the dog but a few times and he'd seen Mr. Dineen almost daily for six or seven months.

No, the urge to get pie-eyed stemmed not from the fact of his acquaintance with the victims of the crime, but from the fact, the utterly incredible fact, that he, Bill Tracy, had planned the murder.

It simply didn't make sense.

Neither, of course, did getting drunk because of it make sense. Therefore, to Tracy, the two seemed to go together quite logically.

You'd have liked Tracy, despite the strange directions into which his logic led him from time to time. You'd have liked him best when he was mildly drunk.

Sober, you'd have found him a bit cynical. But you couldn't blame him much for that; writing soap operas for the radio would make a saint cynical, and Tracy wasn't a saint. He might have told you, had you asked him, that he was a fallen news-paperman.

He might have told you, too, that there ought to be a law against soap operas like *Millie's Millions*, which he wrote. If only there was a law against them, radio stations wouldn't be able to put them on the air, and then they wouldn't hire intelligent people like Bill Tracy to write them, see? So then he could go back to being a reporter.

Couldn't he go back anyway? Well, yes—and no. The capitalistic system has its own compulsions. Writing *Millie's Millions* paid him almost three times what he'd be making as a legman on a newspaper and it take a lot of will power to turn down that much difference in salary.

Four hundred a week, every week, was just too much money to turn down, even after he'd found out what soap operas really were. But at any time of day or night he'd gladly tell you what soap operas really were:

"A milestone in radio, see? And when you turn over a stone what do you find under it? Well, it's like that with soap operas. The sponsors turned over a stone that had never been turned over before and under it they found a section of the population that had never read or listened to anything before because nothing lousy enough for them to listen to had ever been broadcast.

"But they bought things, like soaps and cosmetics. So now they have radio programs slanted at them. And the programs? Endless plays in which impossible, goody-goody characters, if you can call them characters, suffer and suffer and suffer. God, how they suffer!

"To write a soap-opera script, you lie awake nights trying to figure out what fate can do to your heroine next when she's already suffered from earthquakes and unrequited love and blackmail, been captured by gangsters and spies and tried for murder, and had just about everything except ants in her pants, which is the one thing she really needs. But on the radio she can't have them.

"You—I mean I—got to get her into some new jam every time before I quite get her out of the last one, and it goes on forever. Sometimes I'd like to collect a delegation of the dumb women who listen to *Millie* while they mess up their house-keeping and I'd like to—"

Well, that was one of the milder versions of what Tracy would like to do to his fans, but even so I can't print it. Occasionally he would think up strange and new things that would have done credit to Torquemada. But of course Tracy didn't really mean them.

Down underneath, the guy had a sneaking fondness for *Millie* (if not for her fans), and maybe that was why the suffering she had to go through in every script made him bitter, and made him take the bitterness out on the listeners who demanded the suffering.

In moments of fairness, he would admit that the formula the soap operas used was the basic formula of all great literature. The only difference, really, between *Millie's Millions* and, say, the *Odyssey* of Homer was that Ulysses suffered for a limited time only, whereas Millie went on forever, because her public demanded that she should. She couldn't get married happily and settle down, nor yet could she die and get her troubles over with. That, of course, is the real reason why a radio serial must become a bane to the discriminating ear; instead of being a story with a beginning and an end, it goes on and on until it becomes a palpable and palpitating absurdity.

But back to Tracy. After he'd looked at the wall long enough, he went to the phone and called Dineen's office number.

Elsie's voice answered.

"This is Tracy," he told her, "and I've just read the papers. Is there anything I can do?"

She sounded very tired. "I—I guess not, Mr. Tracy. Mr. Wilkins is in charge here now. Want to talk to him?"

7

"Not particularly. But—yeah, put him on; I'll get it over with. Wait, first tell me something. I caught an early afternoon paper and just got around to reading it now. Anything come up in the few hours since then? I mean, have the police found the killer, or anything?"

"No, Mr. Tracy, nothing new. Just a second; I'll switch you to Mr. Wilkins."

A moment later the precise little voice of Mr. Wilkins was on the line. "Yes?" it said.

"This is Bill Tracy, Mr. Wilkins. We've met, but I don't know whether you remember me or—You do? Good. I just called to see if there was anything I could do."

"I'm glad you called, Mr. Tracy. The programs must go on, of course, and I'm trying to pick up the threads and—ah—carry on. Let me see, you write *Millie* continuity. How many scripts ahead are you?"

"Three," said Tracy, glad that for once he *was* ahead of the game. "That is, three besides the customary five that are required. The contract calls for me to stay a week ahead, but I turned in a batch yesterday that put me better than that. Crawford's got them. So I don't owe anything for three days."

"Fine. Ah—do you know Dineen's family?"

"Not intimately," said Tracy. "I've met them once or twice."

"Then you won't want to send flowers on your own, of course. The studio employees are going to chip in on a floral piece. Shall I put you down, for, say, two dollars?"

"Sure. Make it five if that isn't out of line. I'll be in at the studio tomorrow."

He put the receiver back on the hook and found he was sweating a little. He wondered what Wilkins would have said if he, Tracy, had told him, "Listen, Mr. Wilkins, there's something I ought to tell you. *I planned that murder.*"

That would be the end of *Millie,* if he told Wilkins that. Well, not the end of *Millie,* really. But someone else besides Tracy would be guiding her life.

Tracy went into the kitchenette and poured himself a drink from the bottle in the cabinet, and then filled the glass with fizzwater from the bottle in the refrigerator. Those two bottles, incidentally, were the sole stock of the kitchenette besides a box of moldy crackers he hadn't got around to throwing out yet. To date, Tracy had never cooked himself a meal in the kitchenette of his apartment. He hadn't the least intention of ever doing so.

He sipped the drink slowly for a while, and then downed the second half of it at a gulp. He refilled the glass and this time took it to the living room and sat down in the tilted-back Morris chair.

It was a coincidence, of course, he told himself.

But it was a *hell* of a coincidence. Should he go to the police with it? If he did, they'd either call him a nut of the first water, or they'd suspect him of trying to pull a fast one. Maybe they'd think it was a publicity gag. Maybe they'd even think he'd murdered Dineen himself and was trying to divert suspicion by appearing to court it.

Had he any reason to have killed Dineen? Ummm, no, except that the man was his boss.

Not too good a motive. Means? Well, he didn't own either a Santa Claus suit or a silenced pistol, but it's a bit difficult to prove that you *don't* own something. The actual murderer would have, by now, got rid of those little items.

Opportunity? The murder had been a little after ten o'clock this morning. He'd been in bed then, pounding his ear. Alone. He hadn't got up till noon and hadn't gone out for breakfast until one. A lousy alibi that story would make.

Carefully, hour by hour, he went over the things he had done since seven o'clock yesterday evening. He'd written at his desk from then until eight-thirty. At eight-thirty he'd gone downstairs for a drink. He'd had a quick one at Joe's and then he'd gone on a few blocks farther north and he'd run into a couple of fellows from the studio and they'd drunk and talked a while in that fancy little bar that opened off the alley—the Oasis, it called itself—and they'd shaken dice for drinks and he'd gotten home at one-thirty, read a while, and then turned in. And slept till noon.

But dammit, he *hadn't* been drunk. A little cheerful maybe, but not drunk enough to have done or said anything then that he wouldn't remember now. Matter of fact, even when he was really drunk, he never did or said anything he couldn't remember afterward. He might make an ass of himself, but he'd always remember every detail of the process. Not a comforting faculty, sometimes, but nice to know in this particular instance.

He hadn't mentioned the script to a soul; he was sure of that. He'd stake his life on it.

He went into the bathroom and switched on the light over the the medicine cabinet and looked at his reflection in the glass. He looked normal enough. He didn't look as though he was beginning to strip gears. He didn't look a day over his thirty-seven years either, although he knew that sooner or later he'd have to cut down on the drinking or he'd begin to show it. But here and now, as of this August morning, he didn't look like a crackpot.

He switched off the light and went out to the telephone again. He'd go nuts if he didn't talk it over with someone.

But who? Harry Burke was out of town. Less than a week ago he'd gone north for a two weeks' vacation, so he'd still be there. Lee Stenger was on the wagon. How about Dick Kreburn? Dick was one of his newer friends, but he was a good listener and a good chess player, and maybe he could think out an answer for this if anybody could.

He rang Dick's number on the phone and stood there holding the receiver and hoping Dick would answer. A quiet guy, Dick Kreburn, but one who said something when he did talk. He played the part of Reginald Mereton in *Millie's Millions*, and Tracy had written in that part especially to get Dick a job. He'd written it so closely to Dick's capabilities that landing the job for him had been a cinch, even though what experience Dick had had was on the stage rather than before a mike.

But there wasn't any answer and he put the receiver back on the hook. Come to think of it, Dick was probably still on his way home from the studio; he'd been in today's script.

Tracy put on his coat and hat to go out, then remembered he

hadn't finished his drink and went back to take care of that. But before he reached the drink there was a knock on the door.

Tracy opened it and was pleasantly surprised. He said, "Hullo, Millie."

It wasn't the Millie of *Millie's Millions*. That Millie was a fictional character, and Millie Wheeler wasn't. Millie Wheeler was the girl who had the apartment across the hall. The mild coincidence of the names was one of those little things that make life difficult.

When, four months ago, Tracy had rented the apartment at the Smith Arms, he had noticed the name MILLICENT WHEELER on the mailbox next to his, but he'd thought nothing of it then. No more than he had thought of the name of the building itself.

But seeing that name—Smith Arms—over the doorway every time he entered the building, and finding it on his mail that came out of the mailbox, had become by now a definite source of annoyance.

So, in another manner, had Millie Wheeler. He liked the girl. She was as friendly as a collie pup—up to a point, at any rate— and you couldn't help but like her. She had big blue eyes that would have been a hit on television if only her nose was a bit smaller and she took a little more trouble with her hair. And she had a grin that was too wide, or seemed to be until you got to know her well enough to know that she meant every milli- meter of it; then you didn't notice its width.

But the trouble was that once you knew her, it was utterly impossible to call her Millicent, or even to think of her by that name. She was, and had to be, Millie.

And Tracy would sit down to write a *Millie's Millions* script and find that Millie Mereton kept getting mixed up in his mind with Millie Wheeler. Millie Mereton, who was a figment of his imagination, would start doing and saying things that Millie Wheeler, the flesh-and-blood Millie, would say and do.

And that would immediately gum the script and he'd have to yank the page out of the Underwood and start over again. Millie

Wheeler was definitely out of character as the heroine of a soap opera. Millie Mereton was born to suffer for the edification of her public—to suffer and suffer and suffer. But Millie Wheeler, darn her, was quite capable of laughing off the very things that made Millie Mereton suffer most.

No, definitely, the public that suffered with Millie M. would never for a moment tolerate the attitude toward life of Millie W. She was flippant. She was fresh. She was almost everything a radio heroine dares not be.

But right now Tracy was more than glad to see her. He took off his hat and stepped back.

"Going out?" she asked him.

"No," he said. "I mean, yes." He grinned. "You caught me on that one. I don't know whether I'm coming or going, at the moment. Come on in anyway. Have a drink."

She came in and sat down on the arm of the Morris chair while Tracy went out to the kitchenette again. There was just enough left in the bottle for two drinks. He mixed them and brought them in.

"Bumps," Millie said, and she took a sip. "I just came to bring back the cigarettes I stole last night. Not the same ones, of course, but the same brand and just as good."

"Last night, Millie?"

"Sure. Yesterday evening." She took a package of cigarettes from her handbag and tossed them onto the desk. "I burgled the joint. Just after you left."

"How do you mean, burgled?" Tracy's face was very serious. He put his glass down on the desk and stood staring at her. "You mean I didn't lock the door? It was locked all right when I came home at half past one.

Her eyes opened wider as she looked at him. "Tracy! Honest, I didn't dream you'd mind, or I'd never have—Don't look at me like that. I'm sorry, if you really minded. And I'll never do it again."

Tracy pushed the glass back and sat on a corner of the desk. He said, "Listen, Millie. Something funny happened last night —I mean, today. Hell, I mean that there's a funny connection between something I *wrote* last night and something that actually happened today. Millie, I don't give a damn what you came in here and swiped; you're welcome to the whole joint. But tell me just what happened, about you being here."

"Tracy, was something stolen?"

He tried to look a little less grim, and to smile reassuringly. After all, it was utterly silly to think that Millie could have anything to do with a murder.

He pitched his voice a little lower. "I'll tell you the whole story, Millie. I've been wanting to get it off my chest. But tell me first how long you were here and what time. And—didn't I lock the door?"

"It was around half past eight, Tracy. I don't know exactly. I was getting ready to take a bath and go out, and I discovered I was out of cigarettes and wanted a smoke. I slipped on my housecoat and was going to knock on your door and borrow one. I opened my door and just as I stepped out into the hall I saw you closing the door of the elevator."

Tracy said, "Check. It was just about half past eight when I went out."

"I called after you," Millie said, "but the elevator door was going shut and you didn't hear me. And there I was, still without a cigarette. I thought that if you hadn't locked your door, you wouldn't mind if I borrowed a package. I knew you kept a carton in your desk drawer."

"But didn't I lock the door?"

"You meant to. You'd flipped on the latch, but you hadn't pulled the door tightly enough shut and it hadn't caught. So I went in, just for a minute, and got the cigarettes, and when I came out I pulled the door so it did latch. That's why you found it locked when you came home later. Now what's it all about, Tracy?"

Tracy sighed. He took a long pull at his drink and then looked at her again. "If only that door had stayed unlocked longer, so somebody else could have been in here, I'd feel better about it. Now, dammit, I know it was locked from a minute after I left until I came home. See?"

"See what?"

"Look," Tracy said, "I was working on a script. Not a *Millie's Millions* script. A different one. There was a page in the typewriter. Did you happen to look at it?"

Millie turned a little pink just above the neckline. "Well, I took a peek at a line or two, yes. I didn't mean to, Tracy, but I just couldn't help it."

"Read enough to know what it was about?"

She nodded. "It was an outline for a whodunit." She pursed her lips a moment and thought. "It was about a guy who disguised himself as Santa Claus so he could go to somebody's office and murder him, and nobody could identify him afterward. It was a good gimmick, Tracy. I liked the idea."

"So did somebody else."

"What do you mean?"

"Have you seen a today's paper, Millie?"

"A morning one. I didn't read much, though, except the headlines and the funnies."

Tracy said, "Then try an afternoon one. Look." He handed her the first section of the newspaper that had been lying on the desk and pointed out the story in the second column.

Millie read it slowly, all of it. She looked up.

"Dineen," she said. "That's your boss, isn't it, Tracy?"

"It was. Listen, kid, here's what makes it tough. I thought up that idea last night at seven o'clock. I thought I was the only person that knew about it, and now there are two of us—wait —did you *tell anybody* about the script? Think hard, did you mention it to anyone at all?"

Millie shook her head emphatically. "Nobody, Tracy. I'll swear to it. Honest."

"Neither did I."

"But, Tracy, it must be just a coincidence. It couldn't be anything else, could it?"

Tracy said, "If it had happened to a stranger, Millie, I'd say sure it was a coincidence. But somebody I knew and was connected with—Oh, hell, it's still got to be a coincidence. What

14

else could it be? I'm going out and forget about it. Want to come along?"

Millie did.

CHAPTER 2

TRACY, I fear, was drunk. Not that you'd have guessed it to look at him, unless you knew him pretty well. He could hold his liquor. Maybe he couldn't hold Millie—he'd lost her half an hour ago—but he could hold his liquor.

Well, he thought, let Millie take care of herself. She could do that all right. And the world was a strange and monstrous place and there were large and profound things to be said about it, as long as there was someone to listen.

And though Millie had disappeared, there was Baldy, the bartender, as a perfect listener to take her place. Perfect except that once in a while he'd have to go down to the other end of the bar to dish out another couple of beers to the two men standing there.

"It all gets back to the same thing, Baldy," Tracy said. "It gets back to whether murder can be fun. What do you think?"

"I think you're nuts."

Tracy waved a hand airily, fortunately missing his glass. "Utterly irrelevant and beside the point. Which still is: Can murder be fun?"

"Do you mean murdering somebody, or getting murdered?"

"Ah," said Tracy. *"There* is the point. Baldy, with unerring accuracy you have put your pudgy finger upon the very crux of the question. To a normal mind, neither getting murdered nor committing murder is really enjoyable."

"But to a guy like you it's different?"

Tracy frowned. "Baldy, you're not taking this seriously. I

assure you with drunken dignity that I have a normal mind. I have a certificate to prove it. Have you?"

"All right, I ain't. So what?"

"So we get back to our question. The answer is neither. I mean neither getting killed nor killing is fun. But murder can be fun. Ask me how."

"Why should I?"

"Because if you do I will buy you and myself a drink each."

Baldy poured them and rang up the sale.

"Skoal!" he said. They drank.

Tracy said, "All right, go ahead."

"Go ahead and what?"

"Ask me how."

"Okay. How?"

"If you buy me a drink," Tracy said, "I'll tell you."

Baldy shook his head mournfully but not negatively. He poured the drinks.

"Prosit!" said Tracy. They drank.

Tracy said, "And now I shall tell you. Murder can be fun only when it is contemplated abstractly, as an intellectual exercise. Why, Baldy, are detective stories so popular?"

"Because people read 'em?"

"And people read them because they like them. Because murder can be fun—if it's fictional and not factual murder. If you bought a detective story and there wasn't a murder in it, you'd throw it away.

Baldy said, "I don't read books. But a guy tried to murder me once."

"That's nice," said Tracy, "but irrelevant. What I want to know is, do you listen to the radio?"

"Sure."

"What programs do you like best?"

"The crime ones. Like *Gang Busters* and—"

"Baldy, you really *are* the guy I'm looking for. I shall buy you and myself a drink each. No, not yet. After you listen to this and tell me what you think of it."

From his inner coat pocket he pulled out a folded manuscript and held it so Baldy could read the title page. It read:

MURDER CAN BE FUN
A series of 15-minute scripts dramatizing
fictional crimes, complete with clues and
solvable by the listener—

Tracy said, "Baldy, let's get serious and sober. I really want your honest opinion on this. You listen to crime programs on the radio; what would you think of this one? It isn't going to be too much different from some that are on the air right now, but there is one difference and we'll get to it. We start off with the announcer saying—"

He leafed over to the second page.

"—with the announcer saying, 'Murder can be fun. We mean, of course, when it's not a real murder, but one that is made up to test your ingenuity as a detec—'"

"What's ingenuity?"

"Thanks," said Tracy. "We'll change it. That's just the kind of thing I wanted to find out. I never thought of it. '—to test your ability as a detective. The dramatization that follows contains all the clues necessary for a clever sleuth—such as you may think yourself to be—to solve the crime. Listen, and then decide who was guilty. Don't just guess. The clues are there, if you're smart enough to spot them. Today's case is entitled—'"

Tracy looked up. "And then he names the case and then there's time out for a commercial by our sponsor, God blam him, and—Know what 'blam' means?"

"Huh? No."

"Juxtaposition of 'bless' and 'damn' made up especially for sponsors. Know what 'juxtaposition' means?"

"Nope."

"Then why should you? Anyway, after the commercial there's a fanfare and we go right into the Case of the Foozled Whatzit, or whatever it may be. So far, so good?"

"Sounds okay," said Baldy, "but listen, why couldn't you leave out the commercial? Wouldn't radio programs be better without them?"

"Baldy, that is a brilliant thought. I dare hope that it is symptomatic of the awakening mind of America. Anyway, when I get a sponsor, I'll take it up with him. I'll quote you to him and tell him you'll buy him a drink if only he'll leave out the commercials.

"But back to the program, Baldy. We are now safely past the first commercial and into the body of the program, and that's where there's going to be a slight difference in treatment. I'm going to make it funny, gag it up to a point this side of farce by having a detective character who is a dumb·cluck and who can't solve the crime, and that's why it's got to be left to the listener to do it for him.

"All the clues I plant go right over his head and if he picks anybody to arrest it's going to be the wrong guy, for the wrong reasons. It's going to be, I hope, a good comedy script, good enough in its own right to live up to the general program title of *Murder Can Be Fun*—and at the same time provide those clues for an intellectual exercise for those of the listeners whose minds work that way. Because of that combination, it won't be like any oher program that's ever been on the air. At any rate, it combines features of several types of programs that are on. You follow me, Baldy?"

"Sure. But how does the listener find out if he guessed right about who really done it?"

"That comes at the end of the program, after another commercial. The original announcer comes back on for a few sentences after the commercial announcer is through and presents the solution and tells what the clues were, if you missed them. Well?"

"It's okay. *Murder Can Be Fun*, huh? What time's it on the air?"

Tracy sighed. "I've got a few of them roughed out. I'll have to have at least a dozen scripts completed before I can even talk to anybody about it."

"You been talking about it just now."

"Don't be an ass, Baldy. I mean before I talk to anybody at the network office, or to a possible sponsor. And probably it'll have to go on sustaining for a while, and—well, skip it. How about our drinks?"

Baldy poured them. He said, "I was just kidding, asking when it was on. Say, Tracy, didn't you once tell me you worked for a guy named Dineen, who was KRBY's program director or something? Wasn't that the guy got bumped off today by a guy in a Santa Claus suit?"

Tracy nodded.

"Well, look, why don't you use the idea that guy used in bumping off Dineen? That was as slick an idea as I ever run into. Walking right down Broadway in broad daylight masked to the eyebrows, and getting away with it. Wouldn't that be a swell idea for you to use on one of your programs?"

Tracy frowned. He opened his mouth to speak, but was spared answering. The outer door of the tavern burst open and Millie Wheeler blew in.

"Tracy," she said, "I had the darndest time finding you. Were you trying to give me the run-around? If Mike hadn't told me you'd probably be here—"

"*Me?*" demanded Tracy indignantly, his attention successfully diverted from Baldy's unfortunate suggestion. "*Me* give *you* the run-around? When you went off dancing with that gigolo at the Roosevelt? And then disappeared with him?"

Millie perched herself on the stool beside him at the bar. "He wasn't a gigolo, Tracy. He was an insurance salesman. He had a nice policy. And after the dance I didn't disappear with him; I went to the ladies' room to powder my nose. Don't you know a lady always has to powder her nose when she's been drinking beer?"

"You haven't drunk any beer. Just highballs."

"The principle's the same, Tracy. Hi, Baldy, has he been talking murder to you?"

The bartender looked at them lugubriously. "Yeah," he said, "and the program idea's good, but—Look, real murder ain't funny. A guy tried to murder me once, and I didn't get even a chuckle out of it."

"Tell Tracy," said Millie. "He'll sell the story and split with you and then you can split with the guy who tried to murder you."

Baldy said "Nuts," and moved down to the customers at the other end of the bar.

Millie leaned a little closer to Tracy and he caught a whiff of her perfume. "Tracy," she said quietly, "you feeling any better? Less worried?"

"I was, dammit. Until just now Baldy pops up with the bright thought that I could use Dineen's murder—the idea of the Santa Claus disguise, that is—for a radio program for the series I was telling him about."

"Why not? I mean, why wouldn't he think of it, since he'd just read it in the papers?"

"Sure, but— Want a drink, Millie?"

"Thanks, no. 'Fraid I had too many already. Look, Tracy, that ought to show you the whole thing was a coincidence in the first place. I mean, here Baldy pops up with the idea of your using it for a script, and—you see what I mean?"

"Sure, toots. But that's *after* it happened. And—oh-oh!"

"What?"

"I just thought. It just hit me, Millie. I'll have to drop that particular script from the series when I do get around to offering them. All that work and thought for nothing."

"Why?"

"*Why?* Because I got beaten to the punch. It's plagiarism for me to use it now; it's a used idea, strictly second-hand. Hell, and I was going to use it to lead off the series. I thought it was a good one. It really *was* a good one. But now I can't touch it with a ten-foot pole. Who'd believe it was original?"

"Me. I would."

"But you know the sterling stuff I'm made of. And besides, you read the synopsis in my typewriter before the murder happened. So you're different."

Millie sighed. She said, "Also, I'm a little drunk. I think we better go home. Me, anyway. If you want to make a night of it, I'll take a cab and—" She nearly fell as she slid down off the stool.

Tracy caught her. He said, "All right, I won't abandon you. I'll call it a night, too. Maybe it *is* a night. You have to work tomorrow?"

"Nope. I'm off tomorrow. But I feel kind of like I'm going to lie down on the ceiling and go to sleep any minute. It must have been those crackers I ate with the cheese."

Tracy stood up and found that the room was swaying around him in a manner that would have been more disconcerting if it had been less familiar.

He said, "I guess you're right; it *is* a night. There's a cab stand down on the corner. Can we make it that far?"

In the cab, Millie's head dropped onto his shoulder and her body felt soft and warm in his encircling arm. She said, "Tracy—"

"Yes, Millie?"

"L-let's look at it seriously. The script and the murder. It really couldn't have been a co—coindi—you know what I mean. Could it, Tracy?"

"You're a big help to a man trying to forget something. Shut up and let me kiss you."

"Not now. I'm numb and I wouldn't feel it. But I think you're making a mistake on the forget-it stuff. You ought to face it, Tracy. We ought to've talked about it seriously instead of getting pie-eyed. Let's—I want a cup of black coffee, Tracy, and then let's talk it over. I'm feeling better now, a little."

Tracy frowned, but he called out to the driver to let them off at Thompson's, on the corner, instead of at the apartments.

And over coffee and doughnuts he said, "Okay, Millie, detect away. Where do we start?"

"What time was it when you wrote that Santa Claus business?"

"About seven o'clock. From then on until I left. I put the

paper in my typewriter at seven, and I'd pace around a while and then go back and write another sentence and then pace the floor again."

"And the murder was committed this morning, at ten o'clock. So probably the murderer read your script last night."

"Why, for sure? I mean, why not this morning while I was still in bed asleep?"

"Because he wouldn't have had time to get ready, Tracy. Not unless he had a Santa Claus suit in his closet and didn't have to hunt one up. He'd need to steal one, if he didn't already have it—and how many people *have* Santa suits lying around?"

"Ummm," said Tracy. "You're dead right on that. He couldn't openly buy or rent a suit he was going to use for that purpose. He'd have to steal it, all right. And if he read the script yesterday evening, he'd have had all night to get himself the costume, and he'd need that long, I guess. But unless you're lying or I'm lying, and neither of us is, then nobody read that script last night. So, Miss Holmes?"

"Tracy, did you have any rough notes for that idea, before last night? A line in a notebook, or anything?"

Tracy shook his head, definitely. "I didn't. I thought of it for the first time just as I sat down at the typewriter. Matter of fact, I sat down to work a little on a *Millie's Millions* script idea, but I got this other idea instead and forgot about *Millie* completely. Nope, toots, unless it really *was* a coincidence, then—"

He took an envelope and a pencil stub from his pocket. He wrote down an "A" on the back of the envelope. He said, "A. Either you or I killed Dineen, or anyway, one of us is an accomplice in the murder."

"You're lumping a lot under that, Tracy. That should be A, B, C and D, shouldn't it?"

"Yes, if you want to get technical. But I don't believe any of them, so I was trying to get it all out of the way under one blanket heading. Then—letter E, or rather letters E and F— one of us told somebody about the idea last night, and that somebody used it. *I* didn't."

"I didn't either, Tracy. I'm absolutely positive. So next on the list, someone else got into your apartment. Does anybody have a key besides you?

"No. Except, of course, the master key."

"And the janitor has that. Frank what's-his-name. Would he have had any reason for going to your place?"

"Frank Hrdlicka. No, he wouldn't have gone to my apartment. Not without some reason, and there wouldn't have been any reason; I mean, I hadn't asked him to fix a leaky faucet or anything. Besides, what reason would he have had for killing Dineen? And besides that, he's a swell guy. I like him a lot. He's no killer."

"I wouldn't know," Millie said. "I don't know him except by sight. But if he's got a master key, he *could* have got in your place. Or—you might check with him that he hasn't lost the master key."

"First thing tomorrow. Then—next letter; I've lost track of them—somebody broke in some other way. I don't think it could have been through the door because that's a really good lock; a burglar might have broken it and got in, but he couldn't, I'm pretty sure, have opened it without breaking it."

"The back door?"

"Bolted on the inside. I never use it, and it just stays bolted all the time. And my only windows are on the street side of the building. It's technically possible somebody could have got in a window—lowering himself down a rope from the apartment above mine, but that's fantastic. Especially since it would have been in plain sight of a fairly busy street. Just the same, I'll look at the window sills and locks."

"They all sound either fantastic or impossible, Tracy, all of your letters. And especially because nothing was stolen, except a pack of cigarettes and an idea. And nobody could have known that the idea was there to steal. Tracy, this coffee helped a little for a while, but not any more. I'm getting woozy all of a sudden. I—I got to get home."

She stood up, and Tracy had to catch her again to keep her from falling.

They got outside and the Smith Arms was only half a block

away. They made the door; they made the elevator, and with Millie leaning against him, Tracy pressed the button.

By the time the elevator came to a stop, he was holding her up. Her head rolled limply onto his shoulder.

Tracy grunted and picked her up.

His own legs were a bit rubbery, and it was tough going down the hallway. The momentary sobriety the hot coffee had given him was wearing off already, and he felt more than a little drunk, and sleepy as hell to boot.

Millie's hundred and ten pounds felt like two-twenty, at least. The exertion made his head start to go in circles.

She didn't wake up when he had to put her down beside her door in order to get her key out of her handbag. She didn't wake up when he picked her up again.

Millie's apartment was a two-room one, just like his. He had to tack twice getting across the outer room. He nearly fell across her when he put her down on the bed.

Then the sudden absence of weight and responsibility made him sway giddily for a moment, and he had to brace his hand against the wall. The drinks—the ones he'd guzzled so fast in Baldy's place—were hitting him now, full force, but he managed to fight them off long enough to pull off Millie's shoes—fortunately, they were pumps, sans laces or buckles—and to get as far as the doorway between the rooms and lean against it.

The floor of the outer room was pitching like the deck of a brigantine in a storm. As far as Tracy could remember, this was the drunkest he had ever been. Much, much drunker than he'd been the night before.

But the thought came to him—Even now my mind is clear; I know everything I did and said tonight; know I told Baldy about *Murder Can Be Fun* but that I didn't tell him the gimmick of any individual script of it; I know I didn't tell anybody about the Santa Claus script last night; and Millie's the same way—her mind was clear and she talked sensibly right up to the time she passed out.

But that wasn't getting him home to his own bed. He closed his eyes, opened them again, and took a deep breath.

CHAPTER 3

TRACY PUSHED himself away from the doorjamb and tried to cross the precariously slanting floor before it pitched again and slanted the other way. But an ottoman got in front of his feet and he fell across the arm of the overstuffed chair before which it stood.

It was a big, comfortable chair. He twisted his body around and sat down in it. It was a haven in the midst of a storm. He'd have to sit there a moment to get his balance back, to orient himself.

Just for a moment; he wouldn't risk it longer. And even for a moment he'd have to keep his eyes open. In a moment he'd get up and walk twenty steps and he could fall into his own bed. But he'd have to rest that moment before he could make it.

He was drunk, but—he told himself—he wasn't so drunk that he couldn't sit here a few seconds without falling asleep.

But he was, and he did.

It was light, broad daylight, when he awakened.

It took him a few seconds to realize where he was, because the walls and the ceiling and the general shape of the room were like the outer room of his own apartment. But when he looked into the corner of the room where his desk should have stood, there was only a taboret with a Spanish shawl over it. And then he remembered.

He moved a little and found that his shoes had been taken off and his collar opened, and a blanket had been thrown over him.

But the inside of his mouth tasted like a drainage ditch. He sat up, and then stood up, very slowly. He knew, from experience about the midgets with sledge hammers inside his head who were waiting for him to make a sudden move. He knew that the only way to circumvent them was not to move suddenly.

He turned his head slowly. The door of the inner room, the bedroom, was closed. He hadn't closed it when he came through it last night. So Millie must be there; if she'd gone out, she'd have left the door open so he could see, when he waked up, that she had gone.

Probably she'd waked up early, discovered him here, made him a little more comfortable, and then gone back to bed. He remembered her saying she didn't have to work today.

He bent down—slowly and carefully—and picked up his shoes.

The thing now was a shower and a shave and fresh clothes, and then he might feel and look human again. And if Millie was awake by then, he could apologize and take her downstairs for breakfast—unless she preferred to make breakfast for them here. Millie's kitchenette, unlike his, contained the various things a well-bred kitchenette should contain.

He went to the hallway door, opened it a crack and stood listening to be sure no one was going by outside. No one was, but there was a phone ringing that could be the one in his own apartment.

He hurried across and it *was* his phone. He got the receiver off the hook and croaked "Hello," but there wasn't any answer.

He was under the shower by the time it rang again, but this time he made it in time.

"Tracy? This is Wilkins at the studio. I've been trying to get you all morning, since nine o'clock. Thank heaven I reached you."

"Sorry," Tracy said. "I went out early this morning, Mr. Wilkins. To do some research at the library. Is something wrong?"

"Yes. Your friend Kreburn—he's got laryngitis. He can't talk above a whisper. We haven't got an understudy; and there's nobody around here who can imitate his voice well enough to

26

take over his part. He's in today's script, and we've got to write him out of it."

Tracy thought fast. He said, "Can't be done, Mr. Wilkins. Today's program—the whole damn sequence for this week—is built around him. Why, Reggie Mereton—Kreburn—has swiped money from the bank he works for and the bank examiners are coming, and he confesses to sister Millie so she's trying to raise the money to—"

"I know all that, Mr. Tracy. We've been studying it. But what can we *do?* If we pull anything so rank as to substitute an actor whose voice doesn't sound like Reggie's, our sponsor will be so mad he may break the contract.

"Can't we change the sequence of things, somehow? We've been trying to figure it out, and calling you every few minutes."

"Where's Dick?"

"He's down here. He suggests that instead of trying to write him out of the script we write in the fact that he's got laryngitis. But the studio doctor forbids letting him talk—through a whole program anyway."

"Is his voice audible?"

"Yes, if we give him a turned-up mike. But it's not much more than a hoarse whisper."

Tracy said, "But dammit, if he really had laryngitis—in the serial, I mean—he wouldn't be going to work at the bank anyway. They wouldn't let a teller work if he had laryngitis, even if he wanted to. And that alone would change everything. My God!"

"But what *shall* we do? And besides, the doctor's right in saying he shouldn't be on the program at all, for that matter. His throat looks like a piece of raw beefsteak, and if he does read a part today, it'll be worse tomorrow. So—"

"But if he doesn't get a chance to alter those figures at the bank—" Tracy groaned. "Listen, I'll come right down in a taxi. I'll think of something on the way, I hope. And have a stenographer ready for me; I type with two fingers and I can dictate faster."

"All right, Tracy. But hurry."

Tracy was dressed and on his way in ten minutes, and another ten minutes in a cab got him to the studio. But his head was thumping so hard from hurrying that he took time out for a bromo and a cup of scalding hot coffee in the drugstore in a corner of the studio building before he took the elevator upstairs.

Outside the door, he could hear the pandemonium of argument within. He took a long, deep breath before he opened the door.

The *Millie's Millions* actors were all there. They were all talking at once, or trying to. All but Dick Kreburn, sitting in a corner of the room alone, looking like the end of the world.

Tracy looked at the clock. It was forty minutes before they went on the air.

They heard the door close, and turned.

Helen Armstrong—Millie Mereton of the air—got to him first. She grabbed his arm. "Listen, Tracy, I've been telling them the *only* thing to do is use a cutback sequence showing Reggie and myself as kids, as a build-up to the sentiment between us and why I want to help him from being caught, even if he's an embezzler and a weakling, see? I can make my voice sound like a teen-age girl in the sequence, and any juvenile around the studio can handle Reggie as a kid because it would be before his voice had changed, and it would be supposed to sound different, and—"

Pete Meyer—who, as Dale Elkins, was the current hero and leading suitor for Millie Mereton's much-sought hand—had Tracy's other arm. He was saying, "Listen, Tracy, can't we just postpone the whole bank sequence business, at least for today, and throw in some love scenes here? Millie's worried because she's trying to raise that money for her brother and so she's kind of distant to me, and I don't know why, so it leads to a lovers' quarrel and then.I—"

Wilkins, the program manager, a moon-faced, pudgy little man, had pushed his way through the crowd in front of Tracy. His pince-nez glasses had fallen from his nose and dangled at the end of the black ribbon fastened to his lapel. He looked like a distraught rabbit.

He piped, "Tracy, we've got to hew to the line of the bank business, somehow. That's the important thing because it's what the listeners are interested in, and—"

Jerry Evers, who did a lot of doubling, and was currently playing the role of head teller at the bank, crowded past Pete Meyer on Tracy's left. "Listen, Tracy, I can play a money lender, see, for today's sequence, and Millie can come to me to try to borrow money, and I can cross-question her what she needs it for and refuse it unless she can explain why, which she can't and—"

Tracy yanked his arms free and raised them desperately. He yelled "Quiet!" and miraculously everyone stopped talking at once. Tracy winced and held his eyes shut until the worst of the sudden hammering inside his head was over.

Then he opened his eyes again. He said, "Listen, gang, there's thirty-nine minutes left. I can't possibly write a new sequence for today. Unless you want to go out there and ad lib, God help you, we'll have to use it the way it is, with enough patches to fit the emergency. That's all there's time to do. Now somebody give me today's master script, and all of you shut the hell up, and I'll see what I can do to it."

"Here," said Wilkins, and handed him the manuscript. "And this is Dotty; she'll take dictation."

Dotty, suddenly materializing out of thin air, it seemed to Tracy, was a little blonde number with a figure that made Tracy wonder why she was merely a stenographer. Probably, he decided, because—in a larger sense—she *wouldn't* take dictation. If she would—

But there was no time for such pleasant speculation. Not with thirty-eight and a half minutes before *Millie's Millions* went on the air.

He barked "Sit down" so suddenly that Dotty nearly fell into a chair.

He perched himself on the corner of Wilkins' desk and began to riffle through the pages of the script to freshen his memory on exactly what territory today's script covered. Oh yes, the second interview between Millie and Reggie, and the part where Millie goes to try to mortgage the house (*that* part would be okay), and then the part where Reggie quarrels with Dale Elkins and—damn, oh, damn, the whole script was full of Reggie.

He sighed resignedly.

"Ready, Dotty? All right, first scene. Start same sound effects, door and all that. Reggie coming in. Now change dialogue to:

> Reggie (hoarsely): Hullo, Sis.
> Millie: Reggie, what's wrong with your voice? Got a cold or—?
> Reggie: Sis, I guess—"

"Wait," Wilkins cut in. "Look, Tracy, the more a guy with laryngitis talks, the longer before he gets well. Isn't there any possibility of cutting his part down more than it looks like you're going to do?"

"It's just for a few sentences, Mr. Wilkins. Then Millie's going to get the same idea that you got, that he shouldn't use his voice. But on account of the importance of the embezzlement business, she's *got* to talk to him. So she'll make him write notes."

"Notes? You mean, paper and pencil?"

"Sure, why not? She asks him questions or tells him stuff, but tells him not to talk back. She hands him a pad of paper and tells him to write his answers. That way, after this first change running in the laryngitis, we can use all of today's dialogue between them, almost unchanged, only Millie *speaks* her own part and then *reads* his answers—after a sound effect of pencil scratching—out loud, like she was reading them to herself, which she is. Different inflection and tone of voice, so the public can tell when she's reading instead of talking. Helen can do it easy, can't you, Helen?"

Helen Armstrong patted his shoulder. It was a fat part for her. She said, "Tracy, you're a wonder."

Wilkins said, "It's an idea. It'll work, I hope. For today. But hell, how about tomorrow and the next day? We can't carry on that note stuff forever; it'll get boring to the listeners."

"Nuts to tomorrow and the next day," said Tracy. "We got twenty-four and a half hours to fix up tomorrow's script. We got a little over half an hour to fix up today's. In twenty-four hours I can do anything, if I have to. Now shut up and let me dictate. Dotty, take—Wait, let's find an empty office where we can get privacy. Come on."

He pulled her out of the room. They found an office room that wasn't in use three doors down the corridor, and while Dotty jerked paper into the typewriter on the desk, Tracy turned the key in the lock.

He took off his wrist watch and put it on the corner of the desk where he could watch it while he dictated.

Dotty asked, "Shall I take it in shorthand or—?"

"No, right on the typewriter. It'll save time. And I'll watch over your shoulder so I won't go too fast and get ahead of you. Ready?"

He started dictating and Dotty's fingers on the keys kept up with him.

It was five minutes of one when Dotty jerked the last page, with its carbons, out of the machine, and Tracy scanned it hastily before he put it with the others.

He took a long, deep breath. "We dood it, Dotty. Couple minutes with a pencil and—"

He felt like a wet dishrag when he handed he script to Wilkins. He said, "I've penciled some cuts near the end in case it runs long. If it runs short, they'll have to ad lib a bit. Tell Helen Armstrong to do it if it's got to be done; she's the only one of them who can ad lib without sounding too silly."

Little Mr. Wilkins ran off with it.

Tracy sat down and did nothing, very intensively. Wilkins was back in ten minutes. "It's on the air," he said. "It's out of our hands now. I'm afraid to listen. What if it comes out five minutes short?"

Tracy said, "About tomorrow. Will you try to find an understudy for Dick?"

"Of course, if you wish. But why? He's *got* laryngitis now. I mean, Reggie Mereton in the script. You can't have him well the next day, can you?"

"No, but don't forget a day on the air isn't an even day's elapsed time. I mean, a week's scripts can cover what happens in one day—or there can be a week's gap between two scripts. All week ought to see him well again."

"But the bank examiners—"

"Are delayed. The laryngitis is a complication because he can't go to the bank for a few days, and he and Millie are scared stiff. And so are the listeners. But then they learn the examination of the books is postponed—Sure's it's coincidence, but we can get away with it for once. All the other serials get away with it all the time and I've fought clear."

"I suppose it will be all right."

They sat with their eyes on the clock, and three minutes before the script was to give way to the closing commercial, Tracy couldn't stand it any longer. He reached over and flicked on the receiver on the desk.

It sounded all right; he identified the line Helen Armstrong was speaking and it seemed to him that it was reasonably close to three minutes from the end of the program.

And three minutes later Tracy held up his hand, thumb and forefinger making a circle. Wilkins nodded and slumped into the chair on the edge of which he'd been sitting. It had been almost on the dot; Helen Armstrong had ad libbed only a few sentences to fill.

"Tracy, that was wonderful," Wilkins said.

Tracy grinned. "Remind me of that when my contract comes up for renewal. Now what?"

"I asked Mr. Kreburn to come here right after the program's off the air. We must convince him to—How can we be *sure* he'll go home and stay in bed?"

"You might send Dotty with him."

Wilkins looked blank. "I was hoping you'd see he got home

and called his own doctor, Tracy. You know him pretty well, don't you?"

"Sure. I'll be glad to. Okay to use your phone a minute?"

He dialed Millie Wheeler's telephone number. She'd surely be up by now, and if she hadn't gone out for breakfast yet, he could tell her to take a cab and meet him.

But the phone rang unanswered.

"Here comes Mr. Kreburn," Wilkins said, as Tracy replaced the receiver. "You take him in a cab; put it on an expense voucher. Be sure he calls—No, *you* call his doctor for him. Don't let him use his voice at all."

Tracy nodded. "Sure. And I'll stick with him till the doc gets there and get a verdict on how soon his voice will be normal again. Then I can figure the programs better."

He stood up and put his hand on Kreburn's arm. "Come on, Dick. You heard the orders."

In the cab, Tracy asked, "How'd you get—? Wait, shut up, don't answer me."

"Listen, Tracy—"

"Shut up, dammit." Tracy pulled out a notebook and pencil and handed them to him. "If this works on the air, it ought to work off it."

Dick grinned, but he obeyed. He leafed to a blank page in the notebook and wrote, "I want a drink."

"Nuts," Tracy said. "Home and to bed for you, my lad."

Dick was writing again. "Will sleep better."

"Nuts," said Tracy. "Or—wait, maybe you got something there. Rock and rye. A slug or two of rock and rye won't hurt you and just might do some good; and it's smooth enough that it won't burn your gullet on the way down. But no tavern stops. We'll get a bottle and take it home."

He rapped on the glass and told the driver to make a stop at the next drug or liquor store.

He made Dick Kreburn wait in the cab while he went in for the rock and rye. Then he went to the store's phone booth and dialed Millie's number again. Maybe she'd just gone out to buy rolls or something for breakfast and would be back by now.

He heard the phone ring three times, and then a man's gruff voice answered. Wrong number, of course. "Havard 6-3942?" Tracy asked.

"Yeah," said the voice.

Tracy gulped. "Is Millie there?"

"Who's calling?"

"Bill Tracy. Who is this? Is something wrong with Millie?"

"This is Sergeant Corey. Police. Nothing's wrong with Miss Wheeler; she's out, that's all. Tracy, huh? You're the guy lives across the hall from here?"

"Yes. What's wrong?"

"Routine search, Mr. Tracy. We're questioning all the tenants here and we'd like to have your story too. When can you be here?"

"Pretty quick, if you want me. But what the hell's happened?"

"Do you know where Miss Wheeler is?"

"Hell, no. If I knew where she is, I wouldn't have phoned for her there, would I? And—goddam it, *what's wrong?*"

"Been a murder," said the sergeant. "The janitor here, name of Frank Hrdlicka. Know him?"

"*Frank?*" Tracy was genuinely shocked. "*Frank*—Good God!" He was so utterly startled and rattled that he said next the very two words which, of all words in the language, he should not have said. "*The furnace?*" And then, since it was out and done, he went ahead: "*Did they find him in the furnace?*"

There was a pause, a longish pause. Tracy tried to recover the ball. He said, "I mean—uh—I'll explain why I asked that when I get there. But did they?"

"Mr. Tracy," said the sergeant's voice, "you better get here damn quick. We'll be waiting to find out how you knew where they found him. How did you?"

It was hot as hell in the closed telephone booth, but Tracy's skin was cold and clammy.

CHAPTER 4

DICK KREBURN was leaning back in the cab, his eyes closed. But at the sound and tone of Tracy's voice, when Tracy stuck his head into the cab, he opened them quickly.

"Dick," Tracy said, "I've got to get home quick; something's come up. Here's the rock and rye. Listen, you go home and— Hey, driver, take this guy to that address I gave you and then you go and bring the nearest doctor to see him. The nearest one, see?"

"But Tracy," Kreburn whispered hoarsely. "I can phone—"

"Shut up," Tracy told him. "You shouldn't talk, even on a phone to call a doctor. And I'll be home at my place by the time the doc vets you. Have him call me up from your place before he leaves so I can get the dope from him. Write him a note; don't tell him."

Tracy handed the driver a bill, then turned back to Dick. "And don't think this is none of my business, or that I haven't got an interest in that damn larynx of yours. If you don't get over this before next week, I got to rewrite five more scripts! Get it, pal?"

Dick nodded, but he whispered, "Okay, Tracy. But what's wrong at—?"

"Tell you later," Tracy said.

Another cab was cruising by. Tracy hailed it and ran, getting in before the driver could pull in to the curb. He gave the address of the Smith Arms, and sat back.

He closed his eyes and tried to think.

For hours now, he'd been convinced that the Santa Claus business had been pure coincidence. Remotely, possibly, it could have been—until now.

But now—the-janitor-in-the-furnace!

Frank Hrdlicka, murdered by script. By his, Tracy's, script. And *why?* Just because he'd written it?

35

It made nonsense, but a horrid gibbering nonsense that sent a cold chill along his spine as he sat there.

This was definitely beyond coincidence. And it was worse, too, in another way. Arthur Dineen had been just a business acquaintance. But Frank—He'd come to know Frank well, and to know him as a swell guy. A guy who would really—literally—give you the shirt off his back if you needed it worse than he did.

What son-of-a-bitch could possibly have wanted to kill Frank, and why? A homicidal maniac, possibly. Surely no one else.

The elevator at the Smith Arms wasn't at the street floor. He didn't wait for it but ran up the stairs.

The door of his apartment was ajar. He pushed in. There was a big policeman in uniform sitting in the Morris chair; he jumped up. "You William Tracy?"

Tracy said, "Yes. Now what's this about Frank Hrdlicka being—?"

"Hold it, mister. I got to tell the inspector you're here. Stick around." He went past Tracy into the hall and yelled, "Hey, Sarge!" A door somewhere opened and closed and there were heavy footsteps.

Two men came in, the bigger one stopping to give an order to the policeman who had been waiting in the apartment.

The other man was small and dapper. He had a cherubic, pink face decorated by a close-cropped gray moustache. You couldn't judge his age; it might have been anywhere from forty to seventy. He had sharp, alert eyes and the quick movements of a magpie.

He said, "Tracy? I'm Inspector Bates. This is Sergeant Corey. Let's get to the main point first. When Corey told you over the phone that Hrdlicka had been killed, the first thing you said was 'The furnace?' Why?"

Tracy sighed and pushed some papers across his deck so he could sit down on top of it.

He said, "You'd better sit down to listen, Inspector."

Bates smiled. "I can take it standing up."

Tracy said, "All right. I write radio scripts. I wrote a radio script in which a janitor was murdered. In the script, he was stabbed in the back and his body stuffed into a cold furnace. For a certain reason, I won't be surprised—any more than I was to begin with—if you tell me Frank was stabbed in the back, according to that script. Was he?"

Sergeant Corey had closed the door and was coming closer to listen. Watching Corey's face, Tracy knew the answer to his question. The sergeant's face got pink, then red, and was heading for the infra end of the spectrum when Bates' voice said calmly, "He was stabbed in the back, yes. And for what reason aren't you surprised that the method of murder was according to your script?"

Tracy took a deep breath. "Because there was another script of the same series which was followed the same way. And the man who was killed was also a friend of mine—or at least an acquaintance. My boss, Arthur Dineen. Yesterday morning, someone—"

"Gawd!" Sergeant Corey's inflection of the exclamation verged upon reverence. "You mean the Santa Claus murder?"

"Yes," said Tracy. "Almost exactly according to script. Only a few minor differences. I didn't have a dog in mine."

The sergeant took off his hat and ran a handkerchief across his forehead, then put the hat back on at an angle. He said, "Listen, are you trying to tell us you figured out these murders in advance? Or that you're clair—a fortuneteller. Or what?"

Tracy said, "I'm not trying to tell you anything, except to answer your question. You wanted to know why I made what seemed a wild guess about the furnace. That's why."

"But—Hell, it doesn't make sense."

Tracy grinned wryly. "Don't I know it? I got drunk last night, just to forget it. Up to then, the Santa Claus business alone could have been just an ultra-screwy coincidence. But when somebody acts out the second script within a day of the first—" He shook his head.

Inspector Bates asked, "Where were you when Hrdlicka was killed?"

37

"When was he killed?"

"Very late last night or very early this morning. We'll have it closer than that when the coroner's physician reports."

Tracy said, "I was out drinking till about two o'clock this morning. I was here in the building from then until almost noon. So I've no alibi unless it happened before two o'clock. Before then, I can tell you who I was with and work up an itinerary, I guess."

Bates nodded. "We'll want it later, just for the record. I don't think the medical examination will put the murder before two—and probably quite a bit later. And, just for the record, how are you set for an alibi for the Dineen affair?"

"Not so hot. I was home asleep."

There was sudden triumph in Sergeant Corey's broad face, looking now over Bates' shoulder. He said, "How'd you know when Dineen was—?" Then deflation set in as he obviously remembered that the story and the time had been in every newspaper.

Bates looked over his shoulder, then turned back and winked at Tracy. Or Tracy thought it was a wink; he couldn't be sure.

Bates said, "You win, Tracy. This interview is going to take sitting down. Maybe you'ed better start at the beginning."

Tracy took time out to light a cigarette and take a deep pull at it. He said, "I know it all sounds screwball, but here we go. I'm a radio script writer; I'm under contract to KRBY to write *Millie's Millions* for them. It's a serial."

"The hell," said Sergeant Corey. "My wife listens to that and talks about it all the time. I've heard a few programs myself. Right now my wife's damn worried about this here Reggie Mereton, Millie's brother, being short in his accounts at the bank. Maybe you can tell me and I can tell her, does Millie raise the money to cover that shortage, or does her sweetie, Dale Elkins—?"

"Corey, please," said the inspector, his voice a bit frosty. "We're investigating a murder—not a bank embezzlement on the radio."

"Sorry, Inspector. I'll ask you some other time, Mr. Tracy."

"Well, several months ago I got the idea of a series of crime scripts from a humorous angle, to be called *Murder Can Be Fun*. Dramatized fictional crimes, with clues. Not an original idea, of course, except for the treatment I am using on them.

"Up to night before last I'd roughed in three of them, and had notes for one or two more. Then—to be exact, it was about seven o'clock in the evening—I got the idea for this Santa Claus script, the hunch that it was a perfect disguise that anybody could walk around in and not be recognized at the time or identified afterward. I have the script here, if you wish to see it."

Bates cleared his throat. "Was the victim in your script a radio executive?"

"Ummm—no. Well, he was an executive, but I don't believe I specified what kind. I didn't have a radio executive in mind. His line of business didn't happen to have any connection with the script, so I didn't think up one for him."

"The victim in the script wasn't named Dineen?"

"Huh? Lord, no, Inspector. Dineen was the man I'd have shown the scripts to to get them on the air. That's the *last* name I'd have thought of using.

"Anyway, I finished the rough draft of the script at eight-thirty and went out. I left it on my desk, one sheet of it still in the Underwood. Locked my door when I left. I don't suppose—" He looked at the Inspector. "I don't suppose it matters much where I went, does it? Several taverns, mostly, and I ran into Pete Meyer for a while, and—"

"Who's Pete Meyer?"

"Radio actor. Plays Dale Elkins, Millie's light-of-love on the *Millie's Millions* serial."

Sergeant Corey said, "I think he's a drip."

Bates turned cold blue eyes on the big sergeant. "You've met him, Corey?"

"Huh? No, I mean Dale Elkins in the play's a drip, kind of. He talks like a pansy, to me. I don't like—Excuse me, Inspector."

Bates turned back to Tracy. "You can skip where you went Monday evening for now. We can get it on the record later."

"Okay," Tracy said. "Well, I got home about one-thirty. The door was still locked. I went to bed and slept till nearly noon, and then I went out. I bought a paper but I didn't read it until I was back here, around half past four. That was the first I knew Dineen had been murdered, and it knocked me for a loop.

"I liked Dineen all right, but that wasn't why, of course. We were just business acquaintances. It was *how* he was killed— the murderer using the method I'd just originated, or thought I had, the evening before, see?"

"You thought it was a coincidence?"

"I don't know. It worried me. It was pretty hard to believe, but then again it was even harder to believe that it wasn't, if you see what I mean. After all, I hadn't told anybody about the script. Or shown it to anyone."

"You're positive of that?"

"As positive as that I'm sitting here."

"You can swear that, from the time you wrote the script until after the murder, you neither showed that script to anyone nor told anyone about it?"

"Absolutely," said Tracy. After all, he hadn't *shown* the script to Millie Wheeler, and he hadn't mentioned it to her until after the murder. But he skirted the danger point hurriedly by going on. "Anyway, it was a hell of a note even if it was a coincidence, and I went out and hoisted a few."

"Alone?"

"No, with Millie Wheeler, across the hall. Is she still out, by the way?"

"Yeah. Did you talk to her about this Santa Claus suit business and the Dineen murder?"

"We didn't talk about much else last night, I guess. But that was after the murder. Incidentally, she's still the only person I've discussed it with, up to now."

"Did you mention the janitor-in-the-furnace script to her?"

Tracy shook his head. "Not to her nor anyone else. But that's a little different, in one way. I mean, it's been lying in the drawer of my desk for—oh, a month and a half, anyway.

Dozens of people have been in and out of here in that time, and could have seen it. And even told dozens of other people about it, as far as that's concerned."

Bates said, "Getting back to the time you first discovered that your Santa Claus script had been—uh—followed. Why didn't you call on the police then, and tell us about it?"

"Be reasonable, Inspector. You'd have thought I was goofy. Or else you'd have thought I was trying to pull a practical joke on you, or to run a publicity gag. I couldn't have proved to you that I wrote the script before the murder, not after I'd read about it."

"Ummm, maybe you're right. All right, you've covered your actions up to the time you got home last night. And you say you didn't leave here until almost noon today. Where have you been since then?"

"At the studio. I got a call from them; there was an emergency because one of the *Millie's Millions* actors was sick and a script had to be rewritten before they went on the air. I'd just left the studio after the program was over when I phoned Miss Wheeler—and Sergeant Corey answered her phone. How'd you happen to be in there, Sergeant, if she wasn't home?"

Bates answered for the sergeant. "Routine," he said. "We made a checkup of all the tenants to ask when they'd last seen Hrdlicka. And we had the passkeys from Frank Hrdlicka's room in the basement, so we took a quick look around in the apartments where nobody was home—just to be sure everything was all right. It wasn't a search."

"Oh," Tracy said. He felt a bit relieved.

There was a few seconds' silence, and then Sergeant Corey said "Nuts" and they both looked at him.

He said, "A Santa Claus suit, and a janitor stabbed in the back and stuffed in a furnace. It makes nuts, to me." He took off his hat and studied it as though he'd never seen it before, then put it back on his head.

Bates said, "I think the sergeant's got something there, Tracy. It *does* make nuts. By the way, do you know anyone who would have had a motive—adequate or not—to have killed your boss?"

Tracy shook his head slowly. "Nope. Oh, if you stretch that 'adequate or not' far enough, there are petty jealousies and feuds at the studio. At any studio. But none that would have led to murder."

He pulled open a drawer of the desk and pulled out some typed manuscripts on yellow copy paper. He handed them to Bates.

"That's the works," he said. "All of them rough drafts; only two in continuity form, the others just synopses or notes. They haven't been turned in; I had in mind to finish a dozen before I showed them at the studio."

"Mind if I take them along to study?"

"Go ahead. I haven't any other copies so don't lose them, but I won't want them for a while. Don't feel like working on them right now. The way I feel now, you can file them in the waste basket when you're through with them."

Bates said, "You might change your mind. I'll take good care of them. Ummm—this top one's about a jeweler. Know any jewelers, Tracy?"

"No, thank God."

"And here's one about a policeman. Know any policemen?"

"Knew plenty of them when I worked on the *Blade*. But no really close friends among them; I haven't seen any of them since."

"Don't you make carbon copies of what you write? I thought all writers did."

"Of finished copy that I'm going to submit, yes. But there's no point in making carbons of a preliminary draft. Why would—?"

There was a knock on the door and it opened. The uniformed policeman who had been waiting for Tracy in his apartment stuck his head in the door. "Woman lives across the hall just came back. You said to tell you, Inspector."

Tracy got to the door first and opened it wide. Millie was just turning the key in her lock. He said, "Hi, Millie, come on in and get arrested." Maybe he could tip her off, he thought, that he'd not told them she knew about the Santa Claus script the evening before the murder.

He said, as she came in, "Millie, this is Inspector Bates and Sergeant Corey. Frank Hrdlicka has been killed, and they're getting statements from all the tenants. They—"

"Frank *who?*" Then Millie's face went white. "Tracy, you mean the janitor? His name is Frank, isn't it?"

Tracy nodded.

"Tracy, was he—put into the—?"

Inspector Bates said, "Yes, Miss Wheeler. In the furnace. You've read that script?"

"Not exactly, no. Tracy told me about it last night."

Tracy saw his chance and cut in swiftly. "She hasn't *read* any of them, Inspector. And she couldn't have known anything about any of them until last night—"

"Let Miss Wheeler answer for herself, please."

Tracy nodded and sat back down on the desk; he'd got in his tip to Millie that she hadn't read the Santa Claus script, and she wouldn't cross him up.

Bates asked, "When did you see Frank Hrdlicka last, Miss Wheeler?"

Millie sat down in the chair. She said, "Not for almost a week—wait, no, it was three days ago, on Sunday. Something went wrong with the stove in my kitchenette and he came up and fixed it."

"You're sure it was Sunday?"

"Positive, because I remember hating to bother him on a Sunday about it, but I really had to use the stove for that evening. And—yes, that's the last time I saw him, I'm sure."

Bates turned to Tracy. "That's one question we forgot to ask you, Tracy. When did you see him or talk to him last?"

"Sunday, too. He was up here for a couple of hours early in the afternoon."

"Working?"

"On a bottle of whisky. We were playing cards."

"Oh. You did know him pretty well, then."

43

"Yes. He'd been up several times before. He and I played cribbage once in a while, and chess a few times. And I knew he played schaffskopf—sheepshead—so when Dick Kreburn was here Sunday and mentioned sheepshead, I phoned down for Frank to come up and play awhile, and he did."

"Three-handed?"

"It's a three-handed game."

"You're positive that's the last time you saw him?"

"I'm positive it's the last time I talked to him. I wouldn't swear I didn't pass him in the hallway since. If I did, I don't remember."

Bates asked, "Did you know he wasn't a citizen?"

"Of course," Tracy said. "He was taking out papers, but he hadn't got his final ones yet. He was born in Poland, he told me, and educated there. He had a pretty fair education, too. His English was fairly good and getting better all the time, because he read a lot. He always wanted me to correct him when he made an error, or even said something unidiomatically."

"Know any of his friends or relatives?"

Tracy shook his head. "He mentioned having a younger brother in town, but I never met him."

"Why, with a good education, was he satisfied to be a janitor?"

"He wasn't, except temporarily. He was—"

The phone rang, and Tracy went to answer it.

"Mr. Tracy?" the phone said. "This is Dr. Berger, calling from Mr. Kreburn's room. He asked me to call you."

"Oh, yes, Doctor. How is he, and how soon can we figure on his being back on the program?"

"His throat is pretty much inflamed, but if he takes care of it and follows orders, he should be all right by next week."

Tracy said, "He'll follow them if I have to sit on the foot of his bed and gibber at him. Isn't it laryngitis?"

"No, only a bad cold that settled in his throat. I've prescribed for him, but the main thing is rest and quiet and lots of sleep."

"Thanks a lot, Doctor. When will you see him again?"

"About this same time tomorrow."

44

Tracy glanced at the clock. He said, "I'll try to be there. Anything I can do, now or before then?"

"Not a thing. He's quite able to manage for himself, and with the aid of the bellboy service here, he can get anything he needs without going out for it."

Tracy thanked him again and hung up the receiver. He turned back to Inspector Bates. "Where were we?"

Bates said, "I'll have to ask Miss Wheeler a few questions. Here, Miss Wheeler? Or shall we go across to your apartment?"

Millie glanced at Tracy and then turned to Bates. "Here will be all right. Go ahead."

"Your—uh—movements for the past twenty-four hours?"

Millie crumpled a handkerchief in her lap. She said, "Twenty-four hours? That would start the middle of yesterday afternoon. I was at the studio; I worked there until four o'clock, and then—"

"The same studio Mr. Tracy works at?"

"No, I'm not in radio work. A photographic studio, Inspector. I'm a model."

She caught the slightly puzzled look on Sergeant Corey's face and grinned impudently at him. She said, "Not my face, Sergeant. I know I'm no raving beauty. They use me for hosiery and undie and shoe ad pictures. Especially hosiery; I'm told that I have perfect legs."

"The hell," said Corey. "Sorry, Miss, I mean—"

Millie's voice sounded hurt. "You don't believe it? Why, Sergeant, I'll be glad to show you, to prove it."

Corey said, "Uh—I—"

But Millie was already reaching for the magazine rack beside the chair and pulling out a copy of a current magazine. "There," she said, "right on the back cover. The Starlight Hosiery ad."

Corey caught Tracy grinning at him.

He said hastily to Millie, "You worked till four o'clock. Then what?"

"Came right home, by bus. Knocked on Tracy's door on my way in, and found him in a dither because he'd just read about

45

his boss being killed. He showed me the article in the paper, and then told me about his Santa Claus script for the radio. The coincidence, if it was a coincidence, had him up in the air; he wanted to go out and get a drink or two. I went with him. We had a few drinks and then dinner and then some more drinks. Maybe Tracy was sober enough to know what time we got home; I wasn't."

Corey looked at Tracy. "You said about two o'clock, didn't you?"

"I was pretty woozy, too," Tracy said. "But our last stop was at Thompson's, down on the corner of this block. My recollection is that it was ten minutes of two when we left there."

"And this afternoon when I woke up," Millie said demurely, "Tracy was gone. I went out to do some shopping and returned just now."

"Huh?" Corey said. "You mean he didn't—uh—that he—?"

Tracy said, "I didn't intend to bring it up, Sergeant. But what happened is simple. And positively pure. Millie passed out in the elevator. I managed to get her into her apartment and put her on the bed. I got as far as the outer door and fell into the big chair. I sat there a minute to rest and when I opened my eyes it was nearly noon."

Millie made a face at him. "He's an oaf," she told the sergeant, "or he wouldn't compromise me by admitting he stayed the night in my apartment and slept in a chair. It's an insult. But it *is* what happened. I woke up early—about six—and there was Tracy snoring away in the living room—"

"I don't snore, damn it."

"How do you know?" She turned back to Corey. "Anyway I put a blanket over him and then undressed and went to bed. The goof had left all my clothes on except my shoes; you ought to see the way my best dress is mussed!"

Inspector Bates looked at Tracy coldly. "You told us—"

"Nothing but the truth," Tracy said. "I told you I got back to the building at about two o'clock and didn't leave until I went to the studio. I didn't say I came to my own apartment in the building."

"You were evading the truth."

Tracy shrugged. "Technically, but what could it matter? The point at issue was whether I had an alibi for last night, wasn't it? From that standpoint, what does it matter whether I spent the night alone in my own place or alone in the outer room at Millie's? It's no alibi either way."

Bates turned to Millie. "That's all we want to ask you now, Miss Wheeler. But if you don't mind, we'd like to get what you've told us in the form of a signed statement. Could you drop in at my office tomorrow morning around ten or ten-thirty? I'll have a stenographer there, and you'll be free before noon."

"Sure, Inspector." Millie stood up.

Tracy walked to the door with her. "When'll I see you?" he asked.

"Busy tonight, Tracy. Tomorrow, maybe. Let's not make it definite, though. 'Bye." She touched his arm lightly as she went out.

Tracy closed the door behind her. He said, "Uh—Inspector. That part about my alibi last night won't have to be given to the papers, will it? I mean, where I spent the time after two o'clock."

"Of course not. I may have to give them the rest of the story, though. About your scripts, I mean."

Tracy winced. "I suppose I have nothing to say about it. But mightn't it be smarter to keep that angle under cover?"

"I don't think so. The killer—if we assume he worked from your scripts, followed them deliberately—surely knows we know that fact by now. No use trying to conceal it from him. And if we bring it out in the open, someone may pop up with something that'll give us a connection between Dineen and Hrdlicka. Unless the killer's just a homicidal maniac without a motive for the crimes, there's got to be a connection."

Corey said, "Maybe his motive is *Murder Can Be Fun*. A hell of an idea, if you ask me."

"We didn't," Tracy said. "Inspector, I take it you'll want a written statement from he, too. Can I get it over with now?

47

Tomorrow I'm going to have to spend the morning at the studio rewriting some continuity for *Millie's Millions.*"

Bates nodded. "Why not? I'm going back to headquarters now. Come on, if you want to get it over with."

It was seven o'clock when Tracy left the Homicide Bureau, and he was hungry enough to eat the platter along with a steak. It came to him now, and acutely, that he hadn't eaten a thing yet today except the coffee and bromo which had been his breakfast.

Millie had said she'd be busy, but he phoned her anyway, in case her plans had changed. Nobody answered the phone, and he felt vaguely annoyed about it. Now he'd have to eat alone.

He bought copies of two evening papers, the final editions, and over his solitary but far from frugal meal, he read the accounts of the murder at the Smith Arms.

Obviously the reporters hadn't been given much and hadn't been able to do much with what they had been given. The story was on page seven in the *Times.* The *Blade* gave it a few grudging inches at the bottom of the first page. The death of a janitor just wasn't anything to get excited about; only the fact of the body having been stuffed into a furnace gave it any color at all as a news story.

There was no tie-in with the spectacular Dineen murder of yesterday, no mention of the name of William Tracy. He breathed a bit easier and hoped his luck would hold.

From the *Blade,* he learned nothing new. The account in the *Times,* although it didn't rate the first page, was more complete. Tracy gleaned a few facts.

The body had been discovered—at one-fifteen, as Bates had already told him—by a Mrs. Murdock who, with her husband, lived in Apartment Fifteen. Tracy didn't know her by name; probably he'd know her by sight as a fellow tenant.

According to the *Times* account, she had gone down to the basement after lunch to dispose of some old letters and bills. She had intended to put them into the furnace and burn them rather than throw them away. The Smith Arms had no incinerator system. She had opened the furnace door and had discovered the body.

Cause of death was a single stab wound in the back—probably an ordinary butcher knife with a sharp point and a single cutting edge. The killer had been skillful—or lucky—in striking the blow. The knife had entered the left ventricle of the heart and death had been instantaneous.

The deceased wore only a nightshirt and slippers. His bed had been slept in.

It was after eight when Tracy left the restaurant. He strolled aimlessly for a block or two, and then stepped up on a bootblack's stand to have his shoes shined.

There was a magazine lying on the empty seat next to him. He picked it up absent-mindedly and found himself staring at the familiar hosiery advertisement on the back cover and wondering if Millie would be home by now.

He said "Damn" and put the magazine down.

CHAPTER 5

SOMEHOW, HE didn't want to go home. He didn't want to get drunk, either, but he did want to see someone he knew and talk a bit. Only there were so damn few people he could think of whom he wanted to see.

Dammit all, why hadn't he been foresighted enough to get Dottie's telephone number? He could call her up and arrange to do some work with her on the scripts. Not that he felt much like working, but he'd do a little as an excuse for seeing her and then suggest a drink somewhere.

He went into the next tavern and called Wilkins' home. Wilkins was there; even saying "Hello," his voice sounded as small and neat and precise as Wilkins looked.

"Tracy," said Tracy. "Thought I'd better tell you about Dick Kreburn, Mr. Wilkins. He's been bedded down safely, and it's not quite as bad as laryngitis, according to the doc. He'll be back by next week, with his voice nearly normal."

"Good. You've seen him since?"

"No. I don't want to go around tonight because he'd insist on doing his share of the talking. I'm afraid the note-writing idea we used in today's script wouldn't work."

"Maybe it's wiser to let him alone, Mr. Tracy. Ah—by the way, what happened to you this afternoon? I rather expected you to come back to the office to work on tomorrow's script. Or did you work on it at home?"

"No, something came up. I've been tied up until now. But it's all right; tomorrow's script won't be difficult to straighten out; Reggie isn't in most of it. Just a few lines changed to fit in the fact of his laryngitis, and to write out the one or two short parts he is in. It'll be less than an hour's work."

"Good. Dotty will be available if you want her to help again. Or do you work better alone when there's no hurry?"

"Oh, no. I like to work with a stenographer. And Dotty is a good one. Nice kid; I like her."

"She's interested in script writing, I understand. Might give her a lift whenever you work with her. I mean, tell her the reasons for the changes you make. And let her make suggestions to see if they're good ones. Things like that."

"Be glad to," said Tracy. "Know where she lives, by the way, or her phone number? If she does happen to be free, we might get tomorrow's work out of the way this evening."

Tracy thought he heard a dry chuckle over the phone. "But why waste an evening, Mr. Tracy, if it will take you less than an hour tomorrow? But seriously, I don't know how you could reach her."

"Her address ought to be on file at KRBY, oughtn't it?"

"I imagine so. You might phone and ask them."

"I might," said Tracy, "but what's her last name?"

"I don't know, Mr. Tracy. Mr. Dineen hired her; I've just seen her around the studio a few times."

"Thanks anyway, then. I'll see you tomorrow morning."

He hung up and went back to the bar for a solitary beer. That was that, of course. He wasn't going to make an ass of himself calling the studio to find out the phone number of a girl whose last name he didn't know. They might not misunderstand.

He said to the bartender, "It's hell to be lonesome on Christmas Eve."

"Huh?" said the bartender.

"Have a drink," said Tracy, putting a bill on the bar.

"Thanks," said the bartender. He poured himself a shot from a bottle on the back bar. "Here's how. Well, I guess there won't be any Christmas Eve next year, huh?"

"I'll bite. Why not?"

"Santa Claus; he'll either be caught or in hiding. He's wanted for murder. Didn't you see yesterday's paper?"

Tracy frowned. He said, "Just a minute. Want to put in a phone call. Pour us two shots."

He went to the phone again and tried Millie's number. No one answered. He put up the receiver, disgusted with himself for having tried again when he knew she was out. Dammit, hadn't she told him she'd be busy? What was he, anyway—a lovelorn Romeo? Well, not that exactly, because if he knew Dotty's phone number—

He went back to the bar. The bartender was busy at the other end of the bar, this time, but a shot was poured for Tracy and a shorter one, for the bartender, stood on the back ledge of the bar. So Tracy sat to wait until the bartender came back, and meanwhile sipped his beer.

He wondered if he should go ahead and get drunk. He felt lousy, mentally. Hell, it wouldn't matter to anyone if he got drunk. He thought, what the hell's wrong with me; cold sober and yet on the verge of crying into my beer because it wouldn't matter to anyone whether I get drunk or stay sober.

But unless he found someone to talk to—

He pulled his notebook out of his pocket and started to leaf through it to see if any names suggested themselves. It was a random sort of notebook. Harry Burke; no, Harry was out of town. Helen Armstrong; what had ever possessed him to write down her phone number? Thelma; who the devil was Thelma?

Oh. "M. tries for p. lic." What the hell was that? Oh, yes; "p. lic." was "pilot's license" and of course "M." was Millie Mereton. He'd thought of having her get interested in flying, and then decided not to; too much trouble to do all the research he'd have to do to learn the technique and the lingo. Pete Ryland; no, he worked evenings. "MCBF: Mn strgled with own cravat."

He stared at that one minute, wondering what "strgled" was. Oh sure, *strangled*. *"Murder Can Be Fun:* man strangled with own cravat." He'd jotted that down a few days ago, as a method of murder to build a plot around.

He yanked out the page, crumpled it, and dropped it into the cuspidor. It wasn't much of an idea to begin with—not a particularly intriguing way of committing murder. *One* he'd never write. *One,* therefore, that wouldn't happen in real life, as two he'd written already had.

He happened to look up and saw his face in the mirror and it scared him a little. He straightened it out carefully.

For just a minute there, he had almost felt his own necktie tightening around his own neck. If someone was acting out his scripts, why wouldn't *he* be the logical person to try the next one on, if there were to be a next one?

Would someone try to kill him, sooner or later? But why? No one short of a homicidal maniac could have any serious reason for murdering Bill Tracy—but wasn't it the best bet that the unknown murderer was just that, a homicidal maniac? There wasn't any connection on earth between Dineen and Hrdlicka, except that both of them knew Bill Tracy. Nobody sane could have had a logical motive for killing both of them.

And the only link between them, the only conceivable one, was he, Tracy. Right smack in the middle of whatever the hell was happening and going to happen.

"Stop it," he told himself, and was startled that he'd spoken out loud.

The bartender looked down his way, and then came back the length of the bar.

He said, "Didn't see you come back, mister. Thanks for the shot. Bumps."

"Bumps," said Tracy. His hand was steady when he picked up the whisky and tossed it off. "Better give me another; I got to sober up."

"It's one way," said the bartender.

Tracy looked at him, wondering if he should try to talk to him. Maybe a stranger would make a good guy to talk to. The bartender looked like a good enough guy, all right. A little foreign, maybe, and there was just the faintest touch of an accent that could have been Russian or Polish or from somewhere in the Balkans; Tracy didn't know accents well enough to identify it.

The bartender was a stocky, solid man, with shoulders that looked almost as broad as he was tall. He had bleak eyes and big ears. But there was something familiar about him. Either he had a resemblance to someone Tracy knew, or else Tracy had talked to him before, at some other bars. He'd never been in this one before, but bartenders changed jobs a lot. It was probably that, all right.

Maybe, he thought, he should get drunk enough to want to talk to a bartender, and then he wouldn't feel so lousy. It wasn't the complete answer to feeling lonesome and a little scared, of course, but it was something to do. Better than going home. Only, hell, when he felt like this, the more he drank the soberer he felt—up to a point, anyway.

Maybe he should stay sober and act drunk. After all, drunkenness *is* only mental, in the ultimate analysis. Might be worth trying to see if he could make himself tight by thinking about it, sometime.

"Look at the money it'd save," he said to the bartender.

"What would?"

"Not drinking," Tracy said. "Have 'nother."

"Sure. You, too?"

"Me, too," Tracy said. He leaned more comfortably on the bar and glanced up at the little sign standing on top of the cash register. "Serving You—STAN," it said.

53

"Stan," Tracy said, "I got trouble."

"We all got trouble. Last night—"

"I bought you a drink," said Tracy firmly. "You haven't bought back yet. So you listen to my trouble."

The bartender's eyes got bleaker. He didn't say anything. He just looked at Tracy as though Tracy were just another drunk.

It jolted Tracy a little. He wondered if that same look was in bartenders' eyes when he really was drunk and wanted to talk to them. Probably. It was a sobering thought. Bartenders must listen to an awful lot of guff.

And the guys were human. This guy was human; big ears, big shoulders and all, he was a human being.

"Stan," he said, "I was kidding you, acting that way. I'm not drunk. I'm damn cold sober. The couple I had just now were my first today. But what would you think if I told you I planned a couple of murders—and then they happened just like I planned them?"

"You did them, maybe?"

Tracy shook his head. "Would you say, though, that it could be coincidence if you wrote a radio script about a man wearing a Santa Claus suit to commit a crime, and the very next day after you wrote it, somebody did just that?"

"Sure it could be a coincidence. Hell, if you didn't even know the guy—"

"I *know* the guy," Tracy said. "The one who was killed, I mean. He was my boss. And I knew the other guy who was killed."

"You're kidding," the bartender said. He put his hands flat on the bar. They were big hands. He glowered at Tracy.

"I'm not kidding," Tracy said. "The other script was about a janitor who was stabbed in the back and stuffed into a fur—"

Tracy didn't even see it happen. He felt the bartender's hand grasp the front of his coat and shirt and pull him forward almost over the bar. And he saw the man's bleak face nearing his, and the sudden change in that face. But he didn't see the fist coming for his chin, and couldn't have ducked it if he had.

He felt it, though, for the fraction of a second between the explosion on his jaw and the blackout inside his head.

He was in a car and the car was moving. He felt woozy and his jaw hurt. He felt a strange reluctance to open his eyes. But his hand—his hands weren't tied—went up to his chin and touched it gingerly.

"You're lucky," a voice said, "it ain't busted." It was a friendly voice, a familiar voice. Only he couldn't place it.

"Huh?" he said. He opened his eyes.

It was Sergeant Corey. Corey was driving the car, and nobody was in it except the two of them.

"I thought some fresh air'd do you some good, Mr. Tracy," Corey said. His voice sounded apologetic, a little.

Tracy thought of the scene in *Through the Looking-Glass,* in which Alice is talking to a sheep who is knitting, and then the knitting needles are suddenly oars and they are sitting in a boat and the sheep is rowing. One of the best dream sequences in literature.

Only this wasn't—

"What happened?" Tracy asked.

"Plenty might have happened if I hadn't got there. The guy mighta killed you, Mr. Tracy. Of all the crazy—What'd you do it for?"

"Do what?"

"Go there and pop off," Corey told him. "He mighta killed you."

Tracy didn't say anything until he had carefully moved his jaw back and forth once or twice. It wasn't broken, but it was plenty sore.

He said, "I started wrong, I guess. Let's start all over, Sergeant. Where am I?"

"In my car."

"And how did I get here?"

"I put you here, when I saw you needed some fresh air. Maybe a drink would help you, too, huh?"

"Got one?"

"There's a pint in the glove compartment. Help yourself."

Tracy helped himself. He screwed the cap on again, but didn't put away the bottle.

"Now," he said, "the next step. What'd he hit me for?"

"He thought you done it," Corey explained, sounding very reasonable. "He was gonna hold you and call a copper, only he mighta worked on you a bit first. So I guess it was a good thing I was there."

"He thought I done—did *what?*"

"Killed his brother, of course."

"Who?"

"Stanislaus, the bartender. Stan Hrdlicka." Corey slowed down the car. "Mean to sit there and tell me you didn't know who he was?"

"I don't believe it," Tracy said.

Corey grunted. "Go ahead and don't. He is."

"It's not possible. I remember now Frank once mentioned his brother tended bar. But that out of all the bartenders in town I'd pick—Say, Corey!"

"Yeah?"

"You see what this proves?"

"What?"

"It proves—to my feeble mind—that it's utterly impossible that those murders and the scripts constituted a coincidence."

"How do you figure that, Mr. Tracy?"

"Look, my happening to pick Frank's brother, out of all the bartenders in town, *was* a genuine coincidence. It couldn't have been anything else; nobody steered me there. I just wandered in, at random, on the loose. Now if the other business was a coincidence, that'd make—well, three coincidences, if you try to figure each of the two murders as just happening to be like a script I wrote. Now I'll concede one coincidence—I've got to —but you can't have three of them in that short an order. It's like parlaying three long shots at the track."

"I tried that once," Corey said. "I didn't win. But hell, I'd have been rich if they all had come in." He paused a moment.

Then he said, "One of 'em did win. I see what you mean, I guess."

Tracy looked out and saw they were heading south on Amsterdam. He asked, "Where we going?"

Corey slowed down again. "Uh—nowhere. I was just driving around to get you some fresh air, that's all. Any place you want to go, Mr. Tracy?"

"I don't—Say, Sergeant, how did *you* happen to be there?"

"I was following you, kind of. I got back to the bureau about the time you left, and—well, I just kind of followed you."

"Oh," Tracy said.

Corey said, "I didn't mean—uh—" His voice sounded embarrassed. Tracy looked at his face, and it was embarrassment.

"It wasn't business," Corey said. "I mean, I wasn't tailing you, exactly. I just wanted to talk to you."

"I don't get it," Tracy said, honestly puzzled. "You mean you followed me from the time I left the station? While I ate and got a shine and then went into the tavern—"

Corey nodded. "I was waiting. I was going to pick the right —uh—psychological moment. It was something personal, so I was just waiting."

"Until what? Until I got tight?"

"N-no, not that. I did have in mind to wait till you stopped for a drink after eating, though. Then I was going to pretend tò run into you accidental like. But what happened was you went in the Silver Dollar, and I knew this Hrdlicka worked there—because I talked to him this afternoon while you were at the station with the inspector—and I figured you wanted to talk to him privately about his brother. So I waited instead of going in right away. I waited across the street awhile and then went up to the window to be sure you were still there, and I was looking in when he pulled you halfway across the bar and—"

"Don't remind me," said Tracy. He rubbed his jaw gently and wondered if his chin was going to be too sore to shave. Maybe he'd have to raise a goatee.

He got out a cigarette and lighted it, and then said, "Well,

57

Sergeant, I don't know whether this is the psychological moment or not—but what the hell is it you wanted to talk about?"

"It's about radio. Lookit, Mr. Tracy, I—well, I always wondered whether I could get into it someday. Radio acting, I mean. My wife—lots of people tell me I got a good voice. Not for singing, I don't mean; I can't carry a tune any farther'n I could throw a squad car.

"But when I was a kid, I took elocution lessons, and used to be pretty good at reciting stuff. What do you think, Mr. Tracy, is there a chance, I could get a tryout?"

"Well—I don't—"

"Y'see, I wanted to ask you about that—you don't need to answer right away—and then I wanted to ask you about *Millie's Millions*, too. I was talking to my wife over the phone and she got all excited when she learned I'd met the guy who wrote it. She wanted me to pump you what's going to happen about this bank shortage business. And other stuff."

He grinned suddenly. "That's my excuse for getting home late tonight, if I do. My wife'll think I'm in good company if I'm with you, see? Anyway, if I give her some advance dope on *Millie's Millions*. That's a swell serial, Mr. Tracy."

"You listen to it, too?"

"Whenever I can. That's not all the time because I work kind of screwy hours, sometimes all night and then off the next day, so when I'm home at that time of day I listen, if I'm awake. If I miss some days, like today, my wife tells me what happened. What did happen today, by the way?"

"Reggie got laryngitis."

"The hell," said Corey. "That's going to complicate things plenty, what with that shortage at the bank. And the examiners coming. How bad's he got it?"

"He'll be all right next week," Tracy said. "You heard me talking to the doc over the phone from my place. Remember?"

"Huh?"

Tracy laughed. "My fault, Sarge; I was talking about the actor who plays Reggie. He's got a sore throat, and that's why

58

I had to give Reggie Mereton laryngitis in the script. He couldn't talk if the actor who plays the role couldn't, see?"

"Oh, sure. But if he's sick, how's he going to square things at the bank, even if he and Millie can raise the dough to cover it?"

"Well—Say, Sarge, where are we going?"

"I was sort of heading toward Mamie's Place. Nice quiet spot to talk, and the drinks are good. Okay?"

"Mamie's Place it is. Drive on, Macduff."

"But how's he going to get the dough back into the bank before the examiners come?"

"Confidentially, Sarge, I don't know."

"You don't *know*? And you *write* it? You're kidding me, Mr. Tracy. Say, I bet I know how it is. They're shorthanded at the bank, and Millie offers to help out while Reggie's sick, because she isn't doing anything right now anyway, and she's had experience as a cashier—wasn't that about a year ago?—so she takes over his job there. And *she* tries to put the money back. And then—say, I'll bet you know what trouble's coming up from that!

"This here other teller—the one Reggie hates—I'll bet he catches Millie at putting the money back or fixing up the books, and he's kind of stuck on Millie, isn't he? So how's this for a guess? He'll try to blackmail Millie into marrying him so he won't give Reggie away and get him sent to jail. So that's how the next trouble Millie's going to be in will start, even before she gets the last one fixed up altogether. Is that a good guess, Mr. Tracy?"

Tracy took a deep breath and le it out slowly. He fumbled out a cigarette and lighted it.

He said, "Sergeant Corey, you are a genius."

"You're kidding me, Mr. Tracy."

"Tracy to you; forget this mister business, Sarge. How far to Mamie's Place?"

"Two more blocks is all. We're almost there."

"Then don't spare the horses. We're in for a large evening. Your wife won't know you when you get home."

59

"Swell."

"Exactly. And I shall hold forth at length on your chances of getting into radio, and how to go about it. And you, Sarge, you keep right on guessing things that are going to happen in *Millie's Millions*."

And that was the night of the second day.

The following day was Thursday. Tracy's alarm clock yanked him out at nine o'clock. He groaned and kept his eyes open, knowing that if he closed them again, he was gone. Outside, it was raining hard.

He got to the studio at ten-fifteen, which was pretty good time for the shape he was in.

Wilkins looked worried. "I just called your number, Tracy. When nobody answered I hoped you were on your way."

Tracy said, "There's plenty of time. Got a swell idea, Mr. Wilkins—even if it wasn't my own. A friend of mine suggested it last night. Listen." He gave a quick outline of Corey's guess as to what was going to happen.

Wilkins took off his pince-nez glasses and polished them thoughtfully. Then he said, "I'm afraid not. We can't use it, Mr. Tracy."

"What? Why not?"

"Millie is our heroine. She can't commit an illegal act, like finagling with the money and the accounts at a bank. It makes her an—ah—accessory to the crime her brother committed. Our sponsor would not like it."

"That's silly. She's putting the money *back;* she isn't swiping it."

"But she'd have to tamper with the accounts. You've already revealed that Reggie falsified some of them to cover his—ah—peculation temporarily. Putting the money back would be futile unless she tampered with the accounts also. And the heroine of a serial can't do that, of course. By the way, what happened to your chin?"

Tracy said bitterly, "I ran into a Pole. The hell with my chin, Wilkins. I think you're wrong on this. Hell, isn't Millie involved just the same if she raises the money for Reggie to put

60

back? She knows he did it; that makes her an accomplice anyway. It's just a matter of degree, dammit."

"Of course, but degree can be important. There isn't any such thing as absolute perfection, of course, but a serial's heroine must come as near to it as is practicable. Nothing can be perfect."

"Except our sponsor's product."

"I'm serious, Mr. Tracy. Now take the biological urge—"

"Huh?" Tracy opened his eyes a little wider to stare at the program manager. He hadn't thought Wilkins would know a biological urge from an opium yen. In fact, if there were any little Wilkinses—which, as far as he knew, there weren't— Tracy would have suspected parthenogenesis. "The what?"

"The biological urge," Wilkins repeated firmly. "I mean, of course, in the broader sense, and applied to radio serial heroines, to illustrate what I meant about things being a matter of degree. What I started out to say was that kissing a man and— ah—having more intimate relations with him is also only a matter of degree."

"Quite a few degrees."

"Yet both are manifestations of the—ah—biological urge, and the heroine can do one but not the other."

Tracy grinned. "Even if she's married?"

"In that case," Wilkins explained seriously, "the more intimate relations could be assumed, but not—ah—put on the air."

"I suppose not. But what's that got to do with the bank business?"

"Purely an analogy, Mr. Tracy. If you'd been less interested in being facetious, you'd have seen the point. Raising money to give Reggie is one thing; attempting to forge entries in bank accounts is another. Don't you see the difference in degree?"

Tracy sighed. "I see what you mean, but I can't say I agree. Can't we put it up to our sponsor?"

"I fear not; he's on a hunting trip in Maine. I'm afraid you'll have to take my word for it."

Tracy sighed again. He said, "You're the boss. Okay, so we'll have to go back to doctoring up the current scripts and stalling

61

things along till Dick gets back. I'll have to have the bank examiners postpone their visit—which is strictly an act-of-God gimmick and I hate it. But today's script will be easy, anyway."

"Of course. And what is your next sequence going to be, after the bank business is cleared up?"

"I haven't an idea. I'll put one on the fire to simmer, as soon as today's script is out of the way. Maybe I can work the black-mail idea just the same if the villainous teller catches Reggie in the act instead of Millie. Won't be as strong, though. By the way, when is Dineen's funeral?"

"Tomorrow afternoon. From his home in Queens. You know where it is?"

"Yes, I was out there once. I'm going to try to make the funeral. By the way, is Dotty around? Might as well get today's script over with."

Dotty was ready and waiting. Tracy took her to the same office they'd used the day before, and got to work.

Revamping the script wasn't as easy as he figured it would be, but there wasn't quite such a rush this time, so it didn't matter so much.

On a few doubtful points, Dotty made suggestions. They were intelligent ones. After about the third of these, Tracy looked at her in surprise.

He said, "Wilkins said you wanted to write. But he didn't tell me you really could. Can you?"

She dimpled at him. "I hope so, Mr. Tracy. It's my real am-bition, to write radio scripts. It's why I got a job here, so I could be near real writers, like you, and learn from them. I wonder if sometime you'd like to look over some of the scripts I've tried on my own, and if you'd tell me what you think of them?"

Tracy, of course, said he'd be glad to.

There is one thing to be said about all male writers—at least those under eighty—whether they write fiction, fact, continuity, or what have you. They are always willing to extend a helping hand to the neophyte—if the neophyte is of the opposite gender and looks as though she belongs in the front row of the Follies.

And Tracy, being no exception to the rule, found himself with a date for the following evening, and with a slight ringing sensation inside his head that he might have interpreted as a warning gong, but didn't.

They finished a little after eleven-thirty, and Tracy took the script into Wilkins' office.

Wilkins skimmed through it hastily. When he finished, he nodded.

"It's fine," he said. "Did Dotty—ah—make any suggestions? Good ones, I mean."

"Yes," Tracy told him. "She made several, and they were all good. Maybe she really can write. Have you seen anything she's done?"

"No, but Mr. Dineen told me that she has sold a few short stories—I believe he said it was to the love pulp magazines. So she must have some ability. It will be mostly a matter, for her, of learning radio technique. The tricks of the trade, as it were."

"I'll do my best," Tracy told him. He turned to go.

"Ah—just a moment, Mr. Tracy. There is one thing you undoubtedly know, but I hope you will forgive me for reminding you of it."

"I'll do my best. What do I forgive?"

"KRBY is very strict about—ah—one thing. We do not approve of any official or actor or writer taking advantage—ah—socially—of any contacts he may make at the studio."

For a second Tracy didn't get it. Then he said, "I take it, Mr. Wilkins, that you refer to the biological urge? I can assure you Mr. Wilkins, that no character in any radio program I write would think of doing such a thing."

He closed the door gently but firmly behind him.

CHAPTER 6

TRACY STOPPED in the washroom to straighten his tie and comb his hair before he went back to the office where he'd left Dotty.

"Mr. Wilkins like it?" she asked him.

Tracy held up his hand, thumb and forefinger forming a circle. "On the beam," he said. "What are you typing now?"

"I hope you won't mind, Mr. Tracy. I thought I'd start—just tentatively—a rewrite of tomorrow's script. Even if I do it wrong, it might help a little. And then when you do it, I can see what's wrong with mine. Do you mind?"

"Go right ahead," Tracy told her. "Will it make you nervous if I watch over your shoulder?"

"Not at all. You're awfully kind, Mr. Tracy."

"I'm swell," he admitted. "But leave off the mister, huh? Tracy, to you."

He pulled up a chair behind hers. He watched the paper in the typewriter for a while, and then things began to distract him. Dotty's perfume, for one thing. Her left ear, for another. It was a beautiful, tender-looking little ear that peeped out coyly below her soft blonde hair. As he sat there with his chin just behind her shoulder, the ear was only a few inches from his face and he wanted, very badly, to lean forward a few inches and kiss it. Or better still, to nibble on it gently.

But that would hardly do. Ear-nibbling, even ear-kissing, is a rather advanced step for the first pass one makes at a girl. But a kiss on the soft nape of her neck—maybe he could get away with that. Nothing like finding out, anyway. And nothing like establishing their friendship on a firm non-Platonic basis at the first reasonable opportunity.

Yes, he'd chance it. Right there where the soft little golden tendrils of hair started to sweep upward.

He did.

Dotty didn't duck, nor did she turn around. She said, "What do you think we should do with *this* line, where Millie says to her mother, 'There goes Dale,' and then yells out the window for Dale to come in. Don't you think it's out of character for Millie to yell?"

"Huh?" said Tracy. It took him seconds to get his mind back on the script, and when it did get there, it refused to give him an answer to the question.

He said, "What would you do, if you were writing it?"

"I'd have her say, 'There goes Dale. I wonder if—' And then, 'Oh, good; he's looking this way.' Then the sound effect of a window being raised, and then, faintly, his footsteps as he comes up closer, to where she can call to him without yelling, 'Dale, can you come in a minute? We want to talk to you.' "

"Not bad," Tracy said. "Go ahead."

"I think I can improve the wording a little. Like this—"

The typewriter keys clicked under her fingers, and Tracy read the result. He said, "That's got it. Fine."

He walked over to the window and stood looking out. Dammit, just by ignoring that kiss on the back of her neck, Dotty had won the round more effectively than if she'd turned around and slapped his face. Hell's bells, he hadn't even taken her mind off the script. And as far as he could see, she was doing a good job on that script; not that he could get his mind on it enough to be sure.

But, of course, it wasn't creative writing. She might be terrible at that, even though she was picking up the minor mechanics fast.

An hour later, he read the finished script, penciled in a few minor changes and improvements, and said it was okay. And thank God he was now free—for a day or so anyway—to quit worrying about the current script rehashes and see if he could get an idea Wilkins, damn him, would think acceptable for the *next* mess Millie would find herself in.

He took Dotty to lunch and suggested a show. But she had

to get back to the studio, she said. He took her back, and then stopped in the bar downstairs for a quick one before going home.

Jerry Evers—who was currently playing the head teller at the bank, and who played a lot of other minor roles—was at the bar. Tracy liked Jerry, who was the best actor of the bunch. Maybe the only real all-round actor on the program; Jerry had years of the legit back of him—minor and character roles. He'd never hit the top, and never would. His appearance was against him on the stage, and his voice was against him on the radio. Not that either was bad; but neither had the quality that makes women sigh and dream. He could act, sure. He could be convincing in any role except a star one, a romantic lead.

Tracy bought him a drink. Jerry Evers bought back, and then they decided to shake for one. After all, Tracy thought, if he didn't get home early, there'd be tonight and tomorrow morning to think about getting Millie Mereton into a new jam.

He lifted his third drink. "To crime," he said.

Jerry clicked glasses. "To murder, Tracy."

"Huh?"

Jerry grinned at him. A funny kind of grin. He said, "And may you always find it fun."

Tracy hadn't been set for it, and he dropped his glass.

The crash of it on the bar made Jerry Evers jump and slosh out part of his own drink. He said, "What the hell, Tracy?"

Tracy said, "Sorry, Jerry. I'm jittery as the devil. But where'd you learn about *that?*"

"About your *Murder Can Be Fun?*" Evers looked at him incredulously. "The papers, of course. I was reading it just before you came in. Mean *you* didn't give them the story?"

Jerry's paper was lying on the bar, just beyond him. He picked it up and handed it to Tracy, and then while Tracy read, he signaled to the bartender for repairs and replacements.

Tracy groaned aloud as he read. Inspector Bates had given the whole story to the papers, and the papers were really making a play of it. Anyway, the *Blade* was.

The two-column head was:

66

DID RADIO WRITER
SCRIPT TWO MURDERS?

Radio Scripts May Connect
Dineen and Hrdlicka Cases

And the story started:

William Tracy, radio writer under contract to Station KRBY, claims to have written crime scripts which accurately predicted the methods used in the murder Tuesday morning of Arthur D. Dineen, program manager of KRBY, and the murder early yesterday of Frank Hrdlicka, janitor at the Smith Arms, where Mr. Tracy lives, police revealed today.

The scripts, according to Inspector Bates of the Homicide Bureau, were part of a projected series of crime stories under the title *Murder Can Be Fun,* and were written independently of Mr. Tracy's contractual obligations to the station.

This startling development, Inspector Bates said, seems to indicate a connection between two crimes hitherto considered. . . .

Tracy read it through twice. It was, he had to admit, a fair statement. There was no implication—outwardly, at any rate—that Tracy himself was suspected of any connection with the crimes. And Millie Wheeler's name was not mentioned.

Best of all, there was no mention whatsoever of the angle which made the whole thing so incredible—the fact that Tracy had shown none of the scripts to anyone until after the murders, and had written one of them less than a day before the crime which followed it was committed.

It was fair, all right. He couldn't have given himself a much better break if he'd written the story himself. But there was something—He couldn't put his finger on it until he was almost through with the second reading.

It was just *too* damn fair to him. Suspiciously so. Tracy had been a reporter once himself, and not so long ago. He could almost hear what Bates must have said: "Now, boys, I'm giving you this story—but here's how I want you to handle it."

But why?

He folded the paper and handed it back to Jerry. The bar had been wiped off, and a drink stood there waiting for him. He picked it up.

Jerry Evers asked, "Is it the McCoy, Tracy, or a stunt?"

Tracy said, "It's no stunt, Jerry. It's got me walking in circles and talking to myself."

"I'm damned," Jerry Evers said. Tracy noticed that even when he swore, Jerry's intonation was perfect. "That's a devil of a thing, Tracy. But—why did you stick your neck out? Why did you put yourself in the middle by telling the police?"

Tracy sighed and told him. It took half an hour and three rounds of drinks.

"A devil of a thing," Jerry said again when Tracy had finished. "Uh—Tracy, did my name come up?"

"*Your* name? Why would it?"

"Well, they'd have asked you whether Dineen had any enemies, whether anybody you knew might have had a grudge against him. You know all the rows I had with him about parts. I just wondered if you mentioned me in that connection."

"Nope. Didn't."

"Uh—next time they talk to you, will you?"

"You *want* me to? Are you nuts?"

Jerry smiled. "Publicity, Tracy. I can use some. I wouldn't mind being a suspect, if it got me a lot of ink."

"You're crazy, stark crazy. This is *radio* business, Jerry. You ought to know radio by now. A hint of scandal, and you're on your ear. Not so much for writers; we're anonymous hacks. But—"

"Nuts to radio," Jerry said. "If I could get myself—well, arrested for murder, and get enough publicity I might get a break back on the stage. Tracy, this murder may turn out to be a big story. Hell, it *is* a big story. Once this angle gets out, it's going on the press service teletypes all over the country, and it's going to stay in the news. It's million-dollar publicity for an actor."

"You're crazy," Tracy said again. His glass was empty and he picked up the dice box. He said, "My turn to come out." He rolled an ace and two sixes. "I'll leave three boxcars in one. You're plain crazy, Jerry."

"Like a fox. I'm dead serious."

"But what if you really get in a jam? How can you clear yourself? Got an alibi?"

"Nothing to it. Morning Dineen was killed I had an appointment with my hairdresser—yes, it's dyed. I'm only forty-six, Tracy, but a lot of my hair would be gray if I didn't have it dyed—and, well, even in radio where you're not seen except by a small studio audience, if any, you don't get parts unless you look them. Oh sure, there are old-man parts, and I can quaver my voice for them. But they'll let a young-looking man play elderly roles if he's got the voice control, but a man with gray hair wouldn't get any parts *except* the foot-in-the-grave ones. And with television, too—Where was I?

"Oh, yes, I was at my hairdresser's while Dineen was being killed, and his record will prove it. He keeps an appointment book."

"Then you'd never be seriously suspected, anyway."

"But I might be. I could fail to remember what I'd been doing that morning until I wanted to remember."

"I still think you're nuts. But I'm getting dry; go ahead and shake the dice; I got three sixes in one."

Evers picked up the dice box and rolled. But he didn't even look at the dice. He said, "Tracy, this can mean a lot to me. Can't you see it's my *last* chance, likely, for something big? It'll start as unfavorable publicity, sure, but then there'll be the re-action in the opposite direction. I might even get enough ink to get a movie offer. And what chance have I got, otherwise?"

Tracy frowned. "I still don't like it, Jerry. But—if you're sure it's what you want, okay. You shook a tie there; three sixes. Come back, one dump."

Jerry smiled. "The hell with the dice. I'll buy. Hey, George!" He held up two fingers to the bartender. "Tracy, it isn't like I was asking you to lie about anything. Just tell them I did scrap a lot with Dineen—and lay it on thick. I'll take care of the rest, once you steer them my way."

69

"How can they suspect you of killing Frank? You didn't even—Wait, you did meet him, didn't you?"

"At least twice, at your place. Look, I'm going to build up to making them think I'm psychopathic—that I killed Frank to carry out another of your scripts. What were the others about, by the way?"

"One was—" Tracy stopped suddenly. "Nuts to you, pal. I'm not telling anyone. And if you're goofy enough to want to be suspected, you're damn near goofy enough to carry some of the others out, just to do a good job of it."

"Don't be silly. But I ought to know what the others are— if I'm supposed to have read them. I couldn't have read two without having had a chance to read the others. Come on, give."

But Tracy shook his head firmly. "That I'm *not* giving out, Jerry. Okay on the other angle. Next time I see Corey or Bates, I'll tell 'em you and Dineen were enemies. That far I'll go, no farther. Okay?"

"Wonderful." Evers picked up his glass. "To crime, Tracy."

Tracy shook his head gloomily, but drank. He said, "I still think you're crazy."

"All actors are crazy. They've got to be. Going to the funeral tomorrow?"

"Probably. Are you?"

Jerry Evers said, "I'm stuck. Helen Armstrong asked me to go with her; she didn't want to go alone and I don't blame her for that. She's taking it pretty well."

"Huh? You mean that Helen and—Dineen—"

Evers smiled. "How do you think she got to be Millie Mereton, Tracy? She can't act for sour apples. But say—if you didn't already know that, *don't* tell the police. It might distract them from what I want to be their next objective. Namely, me. Unless—"

"Unless what?"

"Tracy, it's brilliant. I'm going to let them think I'm in love with Helen. Then that's another motive for me, besides the scraps I've had with Dineen about parts on the air. Sure, tell 'em about Helen and Dineen."

"Tell 'em yourself. I don't even know it."

Tracy signaled to George. He said, "The more I think about this, the less I like it."

"Then don't think about it. Tracy, was Helen ever up to your place?"

"Once, with Pete Meyer. I had Millie Wheeler in and we played bridge. Why?"

"Just wondered. Uh—Tracy—"

"What?"

"You didn't, by any chance, ever write a script about a character actor being murdered, did you?"

"No."

Jerry Evers said "Thank God" and took a deep breath. "It's not that I'm superstitious, Tracy, but—well, I'm glad you didn't." He stared for a while into the mirror back of the bar. Then he said, "Yes, I'm glad you didn't. Tracy, do you think the murderer will be at the funeral tomorrow?"

"How the hell would I know?"

"I guess he will. Don't murderers always go to funerals? I think they would. Yes, I'm glad, now I come to think about it, that Helen asked me to take her. The police may figure that way too, that the killer will be there. You going, Tracy?"

"You asked me once. I don't know." Tracy grinned suddenly. "If your theory is right, maybe I shouldn't. The police *do* suspect me, and if I don't go maybe they'll eliminate me as a suspect."

"It's an idea. Maybe you shouldn't, then. Tracy, *did*—? Oh, hell, that's a silly question to ask."

"You mean, did I do the murders. No. Which, come to think of it, doesn't mean anything at all, does it? I'd say that whether I had or not."

Evers laughed. It was a rather cold laugh; a bit drunken and —well, peculiar. Tracy looked at him curiously; he couldn't have got drunk that suddenly.

Then Tracy chuckled to himself. Jerry was an actor, and actors are that way. Subconsciously or otherwise, they dramatize themselves in almost everything. Once they reach the point

71

where they are—even a trifle—past the stage where they can act completely sober, they act drunk. They dramatize even that.

Then Tracy quit grinning; he caught a glimpse of Jerry's face in the back-bar mirror. It was strange, distorted. It scared him for a minute—until he saw that Jerry was watching his own reflection there, too. He got it, suddenly.

The poor goof, he thought; he's trying to look like Boris Karloff playing a homicidal maniac. He's practicing for the police.

Tracy laughed, and realized that his own laughter didn't sound quite sober. He said, "I got to run along, Jerry. Got work to do."

Outside, though, he stood still for a minute in the bright sunlight, trying to make up his mind what to do. Dammit, he *had* to get something done on the next sequence for *Millie's Millions*. Was he still sober enough to write?

By the time he got home, he thought, he would be. If he walked, that would sober him up.

He'd gone a block when he remembered promising Dick Kreburn's doctor to meet him at Dick's place. A glance at his watch showed him he'd just have time to make it, so he turned east at the next corner.

Dr. Berger was still in Dick's room.

"Doing fine," he told Tracy. "The throat is improving; he should be able to talk a little by this week end. And if he's careful with everything, his voice should be normal in a day or two after that."

"Swell," Tracy said.

He sank into a chair after the doctor left. "Let's see, Dick, today's Thursday, and tomorrow's script is already taken care of, with you completely out of it. So Monday, if we have to, we can put you back in a little. The laryngitis is already planted, so if you're still hoarse, that's all right. Hell, you'll have to talk hoarsely, even if you aren't. If your voice *is* normal, you'll have to fake it."

Dick nodded. He said, "Tell me about—"

"Shut up."

Dick grinned, and pointed to the afternoon papers lying on the dresser.

"Oh," he said. "You've read about the scripts, huh?" He walked over to the dresser and looked at them. "You got three papers, Dick; I've read only the *Blade*. Give me a minute to read the other two, will you?"

He skimmed the stories rapidly; neither of them different appreciably from the account in the *Blade*. Yes, he'd been right; Bates must have given orders how the story was to be handled.

He satisfied Dick's curiosity as well as he could with the few details he could tell in addition to what had been in the newspaper stories.

Then he hunted for and found the bottle of rock and rye he'd bought for Dick, and noted with satisfaction that it had been tapped only moderately. He had one drink with the invalid and played him one game of penny-a-point gin rummy at a moderate cost of a dollar and sixty cents. Then he made his getaway.

It was only a little after three o'clock; he had part of the afternoon and all of the evening ahead of him for a crack at *Millie's Millions*.

A sudden thought made him go slow, rounding the last corner into his block. It was well he did; two cars waited at the curb in front of the Smith Arms. There was a man waiting in each, and he recognized one of them as a reporter from the *Blade*. The other would be from one of the other papers.

They hadn't seen him. Tracy backed carefully around the corner and went in the back way and up the back steps.

The phone was ringing as he went into his apartment. He answered it. "Tracy talking."

"This is Lee," said the phone. "Lee Randolph. You used to work for me once. Remember?"

"Not by any chance," Tracy said, "the Lee Randolph who is city ed of the *Blade*? Surely not *that*."

"That. I've been trying to get you for three hours, off and on. Got something important to tell you."

"What, Lee?"

73

"That you are a son-of-a-bitch, with trimmings. A story like that one, and we have to get it from the cops, same time and way as every other paper gets it. You could have given us an exclusive, damn your hide.

Tracy chuckled. "Lee, don't you read the books on modern journalism? The scoop is a thing of the past. It isn't being done any more. And besides, I was trying to keep that story *out* of print."

"And a swell job you did. All right, the cat's out of the bag now, sonny, so you might as well give the kittens, too. We got an edition coming out in an hour. Give me a new lead."

"There aren't any kittens, Lee. That's the whole story. All the news that's fit to print."

"Don't be like that. Bates was holding back *something*. What is it?"

"Nothing *I* know about, Lee. That's straight. Listen, though, for a nickel a word I'll write you my autobiography. In six installments; you can start it tomorrow and let it run a week."

Lee Randolph said a four-letter word and banged down the receiver.

Tracy hung up his hat and suit coat, and then went over and looked at the typewriter desk.

It was dusty. He dusted it carefully. He took the cover off the Underwood and put a stack of yellow copy paper on the desk beside it. He rolled a piece into the machine.

He lighted a cigarette and stared at the piece of paper. The piece of paper stared back.

He thought about Frank Hrdlicka. He thought, damn the son-of-a-bitch that killed Frank.

Frank had been such a swell guy. Hadn't talked much, but Tracy remembered last Sunday when Frank had had just enough whisky to loosen his tongue. That was the day he and Dick Kreburn and Frank had played sheepshead, and Frank had stayed a little while after Dick had left.

Frank, Tracy remembered, had walked to the window and stood looking out. Tracy had suggested a game of chess, and without turning around Frank had shaken his head, "Too noisy, Tracy."

"Noisy?"

"My God, yes, noisy," Frank had said. "Can't you hear it when you play? It makes you deaf, that clash of forces. So noisy as hell."

"What kind of noises, Frank?"

Frank had turned around from the window, then. He smiled a little, deprecatingly. He said, "I'm talking silly."

His glass, empty, had been in his hand. Tracy had taken it and filled it. Then he'd said, "I like it. Tell me more."

"I guess most people don't hear. Maybe I don't, really. But it seems like it. Look, Tracy, take a rook—it stands still on a square. But there are—what's the word?"

"Lines of force?"

"Yes, lines of force coming out. Straight lines, with a rook; forward and backward and sideways. They push against any other piece they touch. It's—it's a humming noise, like a dynamo or a motor. With the bishops, diagonal pushes; it's a different tone, a different pitch. The knights—hell, I'm talking silly."

"Maybe. Go ahead."

"A funny noise, Tracy, a curved noise. And the pawns— didn't you ever hear one scream when it's captured?"

A funny kind of chill had gone down Tracy's back.

Frank had grinned. "I talk silly, Tracy," he'd said again. "I guess I feel silly. I think I'm in love. Me, at my age."

"The hell. Who is she?"

"You wouldn't know the name. You meet her sometime, maybe. She's little and blonde, but she has Polish ancestry, way back. I think she likes me."

"You think? Then you haven't popped the question yet?"

"Oh, no. Not till my second papers come through. Not till I'm a citizen. Then there are all kinds of things I want to do. One especially."

"A secret?"

75

"Only because it would sound silly to talk in broken English about writing a book. But pretty soon my English will be good enough to start with."

"I want to read it, Frank."

"I hope you will, Tracy. But it will not be an important book. I'm talking too much. I got to go, Tracy. Thanks much for the drinks and everything."

That had been the last time he'd seen Frank.

Thinking over that conversation, Tracy wondered if there had been anything in it that he should have told Bates. No, none of it could have had any bearing on the murder.

But he thought again about what Frank had said about the pawns—"didn't you ever hear one scream when it's captured?"

And again, as the first time, a chill went down Tracy's spine.

Had Frank been a pawn to someone? Had he screamed when the knife had gone into his back—down there in the furnace room where nobody would have heard him, except the murderer?

CHAPTER 7

TRACY SWORE and got up from his chair and walked around the room for a while. Then he sat down in front of the typewriter and lighted another cigarette. The yellow paper was still blank.

He remembered that the ribbon was getting weak, so he took a new one out of the desk and put it on the typewriter. That got ink on his fingers and he had to go and wash.

He lighted another cigarette, and the paper was still blank.

He pecked out a few words to test the ribbon. Typing always looked nice, he thought, with a new ribbon on the machine. Clear and black and sharp. He looked to see what he had written. It was: "The White Knight is sliding down the poker. He balances very badly."

What the hell had made him think of that? It was from

76

Alice in Won—No, *Through the Looking-Glass.* A dream fantasy about chess. Was that why he'd thought of it? *"And the pawns—didn't you ever hear one scream when——?"*

He yanked the paper out so fast that the roller squealed instead of clicking. He put fresh yellow paper in.

He sat looking at it.

Millie's Millions, goddam it; concentrate on *Millie's Millions.* How to get her in some kind of jam she hasn't been in before.

Give her jaundice, maybe, like that yellow paper? Nuts.

The telephone rang. He answered it.

"Mr. Tracy?"

"Yes?"

"This is the *Star,* Mr. Tracy. Can you tell us——?"

"The *Star?* Who's talking?"

"Kapperman. City desk. Can you——?"

"You want Mr. Tracy to call you when he comes in?"

"What? I thought you said this was Mr. Tracy."

"Oh, no. I thought you asked for Mrs. Tracy. This is Mrs. Tracy."

There was a second's silence. He could almost hear the wheels going around at the other end of the line. Then the voice said, "I didn't know he was married."

Tracy said, "I'm not. This is my mother speaking." He put the receiver gently back on the hook.

He went back to the typewriter and sat down. Nothing had happened to the sheet of yellow paper. Nothing at all. It was still blank.

He lighted a cigarette.

The telephone rang.

He let it ring a while. The hell with it. It would just be—— But maybe it could be Millie or Dotty or——

He got up and went over to the phone again. He picked up the receiver and said, "Mamie's beauty shop," in a high-pitched, singsong voice.

"Huh?" said a voice. It was a male voice and he didn't recognize it.

He put back the receiver and went back to his desk.

The phone started ringing again. He didn't answer it.

He lighted another cigarette and stared at the blank paper. After a while the phone stopped ringing.

He found he was humming to himself, "The moon was yellow—" Only it was the damn paper that was yellow and not the moon and what had either of them got to do with an idea for *Millie's Millions?* A trip to the moon? Nope, you couldn't run science-fiction angles into a soap opera. Maybe—no.

He needed some coffee; that's what was wrong. Maybe Millie was home across the hall and would have some on the stove, or would make some. He went out into the hall and knocked on her door.

There wasn't any answer.

While he was out in the hall, of course, he might as well go down and see if there was any mail in his box. He did. There wasn't.

He came back and sat down at the typewriter.

The paper in it was still yellow and still blank. It leered at him. All right now, the seat of the pants to the seat of the chair—that's the formula. Concentrate.

But he began to wish the phone would ring again. Even a reporter. Just the sound of a human voice. *Anybody.* He wished a salesman would come to the door.

Suppose *Millie* got hit by a—That was silly.

Dammit, was he burned out as a writer? It had been tough before, but never as bad as this. Of course, he had more on his mind this time. Frank Hrdlicka kept getting in the way, and Dineen—and Millie Wheeler and Dotty and Jerry Evers. Was Jerry really crazy to want to be suspected? Or was he being smart? Show business is a screwy thing; maybe Jerry knew what he was doing after all.

How about those old stories and stuff in the back of the big bottom drawer? Maybe there was something there he could use for an idea for *Millie.* One of the detective stories he'd written and never sold, maybe.

He dug them out and skimmed through the titles, remembering the plots vaguely. No, not an idea in a carload, as far as a *Millie* sequence was concerned. Some things there he could use for the *Murder Can Be Fun* series, though, if he ever wrote any more of them.

Only he'd change the damn title, even if he did write any more of them. Murder *wasn't* fun. Frank wouldn't ever marry his little blonde Polish girl now; he'd never write the book he was going to write—and Tracy had a hunch it might have been a good book. He'd never again drink any more of Tracy's bourbon nor play him a game of noisy chess. He'd never hear—

That reminded him of something he'd wanted to do ever since Sunday. It was crazy, but he wanted to do it. He got out the chessboard and men and set up a game on the card table.

He moved for white, then black, alternately. A standard four-knights opening and then down toward mid-game until he got both sides into a fairly even position with most of the strong pieces in play.

Then he sat and stared at it, studying and *feeling* the forces of the men, the checks and threats and balances. The white king's pawn threatened by a black bishop and a knight, protected by the white queen's pawn and a rook.

No, it didn't work for him. He could feel those forces all right; he could even persuade himself that he could—figuratively—*see* them as radiant lines of force, diagonal for the bishops and straight for the rooks.

But *hear* them? No. Funny how different people's brains worked in such different ways. Their senses, too, probably. You could never tell, really, how something actually felt or smelled or tasted, to someone else. No two people, for instance, could ever compare their taste sensations of apple pie to see how divergent or similar those impressions might be.

He thought about a science-fiction story he'd once read, a screwy one, in which a mad scientist had operated on a victim and short-circuited his sensory nerves so each nerve connected with the wrong part of his brain; so that the poor guy's eye nerves connected with the part of his brain that recorded smells, his auditory nerves with the taste buds, and so on.

And a horrible mess it had made of the guy. Darkness always smelled like rotten eggs to him, and a bright light smelled like frying steak; middle C tasted like fish, and drinking cold water nearly blinded him; the touch of a smooth surface was shrill in pitch, and sandpaper sounded like a tuba.

Now *there* was something that hadn't happened to *Millie*. Only Pussycat Wilkins wouldn't like it. Neither would *Millie's* dear public, damn them.

He put away the chessmen and board, folded up the card table, and went back to the yellow sheet in the typewriter. He wasn't getting anything done this way.

He tried limbering up his fingers by typing "Now is the time for all good men to come to the aid of the party" a few times, and then took that paper out and put in a fresh one.

He sat staring at it, trying to concentrate. He lighted a cigarette.

Picture Wilkins with a blacksnake whip. Wilkins wanted a synopsis of the next sequence. And the synopsis had better be good, because Wilkins was going to be plenty mad about that story in today's papers. Wilkins with a blacksnake whip—

"Yes, sir, I'm working."

Try hard enough and something would come. It had to, or he was done as a writer. A burned-out shell.

Who in hell would have had a reason to kill both Frank and Dineen?

Forget that, and concentrate on *Millie*. Millie Mereton.

He put his hands over the keyboard. He hit the tab key for a paragraph indention. Slowly he typed "Millie" and kept his hands there waiting for the next word. It didn't come. His wrists got tired and he put his hands down again.

He got up and walked around the room a while. His cigarette had dropped off the edge of the ash-tray stand and had burned a brown groove in the carpet. He picked up the cigarette and scuffed the hole with his shoe. He stubbed out the cigarette in the ash receiver and lighted another one, and sat down again.

He wondered what sensory impression that guy in the science-fiction story would have got out of a sheet of yellow paper. Let's see; sight had been short-circuited to smell. The paper would smell, to him. Maybe like Dotty's perfume, or like—

Cut it out. Get going. Maybe he could think with his fingers. He put them on the keyboard and started typing "Milliemilliemilliemilliemilliemillie" all across a line and the next line.

He jerked the paper out of the machine and put in another one. He lighted a fresh cigarette. Keep the seat of the pants to the seat of the chair, and—

There were footsteps in the hall outside. Footsteps that clicked, high-heeled footsteps.

Tracy almost fell over his feet rushing to the door and opening it. Millie Wheeler—the *real* Millie—was just reaching a key for the keyhole of her door.

"Millie!" Tracy said.

She turned, a bit startled. He grabbed her arm and pulled her partly through the doorway. "Come in, for heaven's sake come in, and talk to me before I go nuts. I thought I was the last person left on ea—No, let's go to your apartment. I want to get *out* of mine." He shuddered.

"Tracy, have you been drinking?"

"No, but it's an idea. Shall we?"

She got her door unlocked and he followed her in. She headed for the kitchenette. "Coffee?"

"Sure, swell."

"Hungry?"

"I don't know. I don't think so."

"All right, I'll start some coffee perking. Then you can sit down and tell mama what's bothering you. Wait—isn't that your phone ringing?"

He got across the hall in time to answer it.

"Tracy talking."

"This is Inspector Bates, Tracy. Do you know a man named Walther Mueller? Ever hear the name?"

"Ummm—has a vaguely familiar ring to it. Might have heard of him or met him, but I don't think I ever *knew* anyone by that name. Who is he?"

Bates was evasive. "Just a name that came up in the course of our investigation. Have you written any more murder scripts?"

"Hell, no."

"Maybe you're wise. If I were you, I wouldn't—until after we find out a little more than we know now."

"And what do you know now?"

Bates chuckled. "Confidentially, nothing at all. By the way, where did Dineen get that Doberman of his? Do you happen to know? His wife says he brought it home from the studio, that somebody there gave it to him when the dog was a puppy."

"Must have been before I worked there. Wait a minute—it might have been Pete Meyer. Pete has a police dog—I guess it's a Doberman. And it's a bitch; likely she had a litter and he polished an apple by giving one to the boss."

"Pete Meyer? That's the hero of *Millie's Millions*, isn't it?"

"Yeah. Dale Elkins of the air waves—as we of radio never say. But that's just a guess about its being Pete; ask somebody who worked there longer if you want to be sure."

"I'll try Dineen's secretary; she's been there four years, and the dog is only two. By the way, is she going to be Wilkins' secretary?"

"I haven't an idea," Tracy said. "By the way, how is the dog?"

"Okay, I hear. It's still at a vet hospital, but just because they figure it's best to leave it there until after the funeral. It was just creased, the vet says. Tracy, where were you the first week in June this year? In New York?"

"Let's see—believe I was. I spent two weeks in June up on Cape Cod for a vacation, but that was starting the tenth, I think. That'd mean I was in New York the first week. Why?"

"Just checking up," Bates said. "Something happened then that might possibly have been connected with—uh—subsequent events. By the way, have you thought of anything you haven't told me that might possibly have a bearing on the case?"

"One little thing. I thought over your question about who at the studio might have a grudge against Dineen. The best bet would be Jerry Evers—he takes character parts in *Millie* and other serials. He had a blowup with Dineen over a contract. I think he went over Dineen's head on the matter, and Dineen didn't like that so he rode Jerry every chance he had. I don't think there's anything in it—from a murder point of view. But you might talk to Evers, just to be sure."

"We'll do that. Anything else?"

"Ummm. Probably this doesn't mean anything either. But I remember that Sunday Frank told me he'd met a girl he hoped to marry after he got his second citizenship papers."

"We didn't know that," Bates said. "His brother didn't know it, either. We asked him if Frank had any woman on the string and he said not. Did Frank tell you her name?"

"No, he didn't tell me anything about her. Small, and blonde, and he thought she had Polish ancestry. And I gathered that it wasn't a two-way romance, yet."

"We'll try to find her. Thanks, Tracy. Be seeing you."

Tracy stood there a minute after he'd put the receiver back, trying again to place the name Walther Mueller. But he couldn't.

He turned and thumbed his nose at the typewriter with the blank sheet of yellow paper in it, and then went back across the hall to have coffee with Millie.

*   *   *

It was dusk, and there was a cool drizzle. Tracy stood watching as the street light on the corner went on and gathered itself a yellow halo that it didn't deserve. There's nothing holy, he thought, about an electric light—a glowing filament that manages, despite its yellow heat, to give a cold impersonal radiance—a light to see by, not to live by.

He wondered what the devil had made him think that. Hell's bells, he wasn't a romanticist. He was—

What the hell was he?

83

Just now, he decided wryly, he was a guy standing outside a doorway in a thin drizzle of rain, wondering where to go and what to do, now that Millie had given him the brush-off so she could get dressed for an appointment. A business appointment, she'd said. But where did that leave Tracy? *A little black sheep who has gone astray, baaa, baaa*—Bah. Why did Millie have to see a photographer this evening?

Or why wasn't his date with the dimpled Dotty tonight instead of tomorrow night?

Well, he had to do something. Eat? No, he wasn't hungry. Get a drink? He didn't really want one, but what the hell, he had to do something or else face the thought of going back up to his apartment and looking at a jaundiced sheet of paper in a typewriter. And *that* was a horrible thought.

Better to be driven to drink. Better even to walk to drink, if a taxi didn't come along. And it probably wouldn't; taxis always hide the moment it starts to rain.

Better far to—

"Pardon me," said a voice beside him. "Aren't you Mr. Tracy?"

Tracy turned and saw a dowdy, dumpy woman looking at him through wide eyes behind rain-spattered glasses. She wore a greenish mottled *babushka* and the stringy hair that pushed out in front of it was beaded with rain.

"Yes, ma'am," Tracy said.

"I thought you *must* be, because I know nearly everybody in the building except you and when I read your name in the paper and this address I thought—well, it can't be the bald man on the fifth floor because he couldn't *possibly* be a writer, as dumb as he looks, and it can't be the plump man in two-eighteen, I don't know his name either, because's he's married —or I guess they're married—and while it didn't just come out and say in the paper that you weren't married, I sort of got that impression from it, and anyway *he* doesn't look like a writer either, and I've seen you in the hallway and always figured you must be a newspaperman or something. So it *had* to be you."

"Marvelous deduction," Tracy said. "But I don't—"

"I'm Mrs. Murdock, Mr. Tracy."

"Mrs.—Oh, you're the woman who found—?"

"The body, yes. Wasn't it *horrible?* I nearly keeled over when I opened the door of that furnace and—well, you can imagine what an awful shock it was. But, like my husband always says, you never know. In the middle of life you are in death, isn't it so? Mr. Murdock sells insurance, you know, and only last month he suggested to Mr. Hrdlicka that he ought to take out a policy, even a small policy, since being a janitor couldn't have paid very much; I don't know how much, but, of course, he had a place to live thrown in with it, and he said he'd think about it, but he didn't. And now look, he's dead and he didn't."

She stopped for a moment to sigh; it was a brief moment. Tracy opened his mouth—but too late. She was off again. "Keeping you in the rain like this, talking. I don't mind rain; I *like* rain. I like to take long walks in the rain even when it's raining hard; my husband says I'm always wanting to go out the minute it even gets cloudy. But I'm keeping you, Mr. Tracy —Won't you come on up to our apartment and meet my husband? We were saying we'd like to know you. We're in five-fifteen. He's home now; we ate and then I went out for a walk in the rain; he'd be just crazy about it if I brought you up with me. We're both awful radio fans, you know, and we listen to— What is the program you write, Mr. Tracy?"

"*Millie's Mil—*"

"*Millie's Millions?* Why, I listen to that one every day. My husband doesn't; he's working that time of day and he likes the crime ones and the horror ones best, anyway. Like *Suspense.* They give me the creeps; I don't like things like that, but it had to be *me* that opened the furnace door and saw—why, it was just like one of those programs my husband listens to, and that I have to listen to, too, because when a radio's on, you can't help but hear it, and because he isn't home very much—selling insurance, you've got to make evening calls, too—I can't very well not want him to listen to the programs *he* wants to hear when he is home when I have the radio all to myself all the rest of the time. Don't you think so?"

"Of course," said Tracy, rather vaguely, not quite sure what he was agreeing to. He hurried on: "But I'm afraid, Mrs. Murdock, that I can't meet your husband now. I have an appointment. I—"

"Oh, that's too bad. He'd *so* like to meet you. And he *wouldn't*"—she simpered a little—"try to sell you an insurance policy. I mean, he used to talk insurance sometimes to people who came to see us socially. But I put my foot down. Business is business, but home is no place for it, even if I *do,* naturally, have an interest in how much money he makes. Don't you think so? Well, it's too bad; after your having written about it and all, I wanted to tell you just how I found Mr. Hrdlicka and all the circumstances and everything. Then you'd know how close you guessed."

"How close I—"

"Of course. In your story for the radio. But here I am keeping you standing in the rain. I'm so sorry you haven't time to come up and spend the evening with us. My husband would be so—Mr. Tracy, have you been down there in the basement since it happened? I mean, in the furnace room where I found him? It was so horrible and exciting. I wonder if you'd like to have me show you just where he was, and everything; I mean, a man like you who *writes* about those things, you might be able to figure out what happened, even better than the police. I don't like that Mr. Corey at all, do you? And in the stories you read and on the radio, the police never find out what really happened, do they? They always want to arrest somebody who didn't have anything to do with it—like you or me. Would you?"

"Beg pardon," Tracy said. "Would I what?"

"Like to have me show you down in the furnace room?"

"I'm sorry, but—Wait, I think I would. If you'd be so kind, Mrs. Murdock, I think I would."

He took her firmly by the arm and led her into the building. "We'll take the elevator down, then," she was saying. "Not because one flight down is far to walk, but because that's the way I went down yesterday when I found it—him, I mean. I was taking some papers down to be burned, and of course because it was five flights down, I took the elevator and—"

The basement lights were on.

On the way to the furnace, Mrs. Murdock still kept talking. ". . . the papers held against me with my arm, and I opened the main furnace door, this door, like this, and there he was. Only at first I thought it was a pair of slippers somebody had wanted to throw away and hadn't thrown far enough and they'd stopped on the ledge just inside the door, right there. Then I saw there were bare ankles coming out of the slippers, and I dropped the papers and I screamed—Did you have that right in your story?"

"Huh?" said Tracy. He was staring into the open furnace.

"Oh, I don't mean about my dropping the papers and screaming. I know you couldn't have put me into the script because —well, you didn't know me. But I mean, did you have it right about his being in night clothes and slippers?"

Tracy pulled his eyes and his thoughts away from the maw of the furnace and looked at her wonderingly. Was she nuts?

She smiled at him. It was supposed to be a reassuring smile he thought. She said, "You needn't pretend with *us,* Mr. Tracy. With my husband and me, I mean. The very minute we read the papers this afternoon, about your scripts, I said, 'It's a publicity stunt, isn't it, Wally?' and he said, 'It's a damn smart one. I'd like to meet the guy, hon. If he can fool the cops into releasing a story like that, he's a smart duck.' And I thought, and said I wished I'd known you so I could have given you the inside facts about how the body was dressed and—things like that."

Tracy just looked at her. When she stopped talking, he said very quietly, "Mrs. Murdock—"

"Maybe I shouldn't have put it just that way, Mr. Tracy. I didn't mean to accuse you of—I mean, I didn't mean to hurt your—"

She ran out of words, and it was very quiet there in the basement for a full second.

Until Tracy smiled and said, "You forget, Mrs. Murdock, that there *might* be another explanation."

"Another ex—You mean—?"

"It might not have been a publicity stunt. Did it ever occur to you that I might have—"

He let it hang there, and smiled again. She took a quick step backwards. The back of her hand went up to her mouth, and she took another step. Then she turned and ran. He heard the elevator door clang.

The slow burn back of Tracy's smile died out then, and the smile turned to a grin. Believe it or not, he'd got in the last word. Quite a trick, with *that* dame. He wouldn't be surprised if he was the first man who'd ever done it.

Then the grin died as he looked back at the furnace door.

It was a big, old-fashioned furnace. No stoker. A door plenty big enough to put a man through.

Staring at it, he wondered why he'd come down here. He shivered a little, and closed the door of the furnace. Yes, it had been a silly idea to come down here—but how could a man think coherently with a woman like that jabbering at him?

But now that he was down here and alone, could he get into the rooms Frank had off to the left of the furnace room? Probably not; the police would have locked them up. But he turned and looked.

The door of the outer room was ajar, almost halfway open, and there was a light inside.

CHAPTER 8

FOR JUST an instant, Tracy wanted to turn and run. Then he took a few steps toward the door and to his right, so he could see in through the half-open doorway.

He could see the table that stood at the end of Frank's bed. There was a chessboard on the table, and chessmen on the board, half a dozen of them. A hand reached out, picked up one of the men and then put it down again on a different square.

Tracy walked closer to the door, and a voice said, "Come on in, Tracy." It was Inspector Bates' voice.

Tracy went in. Bates was there alone, sitting on a chair alongside the table; he didn't raise his eyes from the chessboard. Tracy looked from Bates' intent face to the position of the pieces.

Bates said, "This is the way they were set up. Looks like a problem; it's an improbable position for an end game. Probably a two-mover. But I haven't found the key move."

Tracy said, "It's a two-move problem; I've worked it out. The key—or should I tell you?"

"Go ahead, and get it off my mind. I should be thinking about other things."

"Knight to the rook's fourth."

"I tried that. But doesn't the pawn move spill it? How can white mate if black moves the pawn?"

"Black can't move the pawn. Moving that knight uncovers a pin on the pawn; it'd be moving into check."

Bates snapped his fingers. "Blind," he said. "Blinder than a bat."

He looked up from the chessboard. He said, "You weren't too smart either, Tracy—throwing that scare into Mrs. M."

Tracy grinned. "Only way I could stop her. Hope I wasn't too convincing, though."

The grin slid off his face as he met Bates' eyes. They were cold, unfriendly, and calculating. Bates tapped the left lapel of his coat. He said, "There was a gun on you until she made the elevator safely."

Tracy whistled soundlessly. He said, "You really thought—?"

"I wasn't trying to think. I just wasn't taking any chances. About this chess problem. Did you show it to Hrdlicka?"

"No. It was in the *Blade*. They run a chess problem every day. That one was in yesterday morning's—Say—"

"What?"

"Just a thought. The first edition that carried that problem hit the streets at eleven o'clock Tuesday evening. If Frank set that problem up himself—and it would be rather silly for the murderer to have done it—that definitely dates the murder after midnight. I mean, Frank must have gone out to buy a paper—necessarily after eleven—and he'd have had time to come home and set up the problem."

Bates said, "There was a Wednesday *Blade* here. Not that that's needed to prove he died after midnight. We've got the coroner's autopsy report now."

"When?"

"Around three o'clock. Between two and four, if we allow an hour each way to be safe. Doc Merkel says, though, it's closer than that—within ten or fifteen minutes of three o'clock."

Tracy said, "That's cutting it pretty fine, for an autopsy made at least twelve hours later."

"Would be if we hadn't something to go on. He was in Thompson's down at the corner at midnight, though; counterman there knew him. So we know what he ate last, and when. Doc says the digestive period on the last food he had was just about three hours."

Tracy sat down on the edge of the bed. He said, "That's when he'd have bought the paper, then. He came home and set up the chess problem, maybe studied it a while. I'd say he didn't solve it, or he'd have put the men away. He undressed for bed and—Didn't the papers say his bed had been slept in?"

"One of them did. It was wrong. He must have been still awake when the killer came. Probably reading; there was a book lying open on the bed, just as he must have put it down to answer the door."

Tracy nodded slowly. He asked, "The stab wound—it was through the nightshirt?"

"Yes. Why?"

90

"Then it's pretty certain the killer was a man, Inspector."

"Probably, yes, but why?"

"He must have admitted a visitor—without putting on anything over the nightshirt. If a woman had come, he'd have pulled on his trousers or put on a bathrobe, wouldn't he?"

"Probably. Unless, of course, he was on pretty intimate terms with the woman. How do we know he wasn't having an affair with some woman living here in the building who sneaked down to see him? Maybe that's what he was waiting up for?"

"No. I knew Frank pretty well, and I don't think he was having an affair. And if he was, damn it, he would have been wearing a robe—or something besides a nightshirt—to let the woman in when she came. A nightshirt isn't a romantic garment, Inspector. A man might wait for an assignation in pajamas, but only a lout would wear a nightshirt. And Frank wasn't a lout."

Bates chuckled. "Maybe you've got something there. Not that we seriously thought it *was* a woman, anyway. For one thing, she'd have to be pretty husky to have put him into the furnace afterward."

Tracy stood up. "Want to come out and have a drink with me, Inspector? Or don't you drink with your suspects?"

Bates said drily, "I always drink with my suspects; it loosens their tongues. But I'll take a rain check tonight. I just got here —before you and Mrs. Murdock staged your little horror program out by the furnace there. I've got work to do."

"Such as?"

"Looking through all his books, papers, everything. No, I don't know what I'm looking for. Just for anything that might give me an idea or a lead. I was taking that chess setup first, because it was out in the open. Now I know it's a problem and where it came from, I can go on from there."

Bates was starting systematically at the right side of the bookshelf when Tracy left.

It was still drizzling rain when he reached the street, and after one look both ways for a taxi, Tracy turned up the collar of his coat and started walking uptown. No destination in mind. Not even any special yen for a drink, although he knew he'd end up drinking.

What the devil had he been going to ask Bates about, and had forgotten? It bothered him for two blocks before he remembered. The name Walther Mueller that Bates had asked him about; who the deuce was Walther Mueller?

All Bates had told him over the phone was that the name "had come up in the course of our investigation." And then Bates had asked him if he'd been in town the first week in June.

Had there been any connection between the two questions: the name and the date? If so—

At the next corner he turned east, and three blocks found him at the *Blade* building. He avoided the main entrance and went back by way of the loading platform to the door that led to the circulation department.

Ray Beckman, night circulation man, was working on a report. He looked up and said, "Hi, Tracy. Want a job as newsboy?"

"Might try a route if you got one open. Say, Ray, you got a key to the stack room?"

"Sure. Want something?"

"Could you get me a set of copies for the first week in June?"

"Sure. Stick around."

Beckman went down the hall and came back a few minutes later with a stack of papers.

Tracy tucked them under his arm. "Thanks, Ray. Time to sneak out for a quickie?"

Beckman looked at the clock and shook his head regretfully. "Trucks are just about due for the upstate edition. I'll take a rain check. Why don't you ever drop around at Barney's any more?"

"Going there now," Tracy said. "I'll stick around an hour or so in case you can shake loose."

Before he left the building, he went to the door of the pressroom and stood there awhile. The two enormous rotaries, each

92

over a hundred feet long, were rolling. It had been a long time now since Tracy had watched them, but—as always—they hypnotized him a little.

Thunder, and the smell of fresh ink. The dizzily spinning rollers and the endless white paper.

He shook it off after a minute and went outside again, and around the corner to Barney's.

Barney came along the bar and stared at him. He said, "If my eyes ain't lying, it's Tracy. Long time no see."

"Long time no drink," Tracy said. "Blue Label, Barney. And how's business?"

"Not the same since you quit working."

"Quit working, hell. I'll have you know that—"

But Barney was already down near the other end of the bar looking for the Blue Label bottle.

Over his second drink, Tracy started on his first paper from the stack of seven on the stool beside him. The first time through, he would read only the headlines, he decided. If that didn't give him what he wanted, he'd have to take the papers slower for a second reading, and dip into the minion.

There wasn't any headline in the first paper that sounded to the point. Nor in the second or third.

Barney came back as he was reaching for the fourth paper. He said, "On the house, Tracy," and refilled the shot glass from the Blue Label bottle. "No kidding, Tracy," he said, "one of the boys told me you were working for a whorehouse. Where is it?"

Tracy had started to lift the drink. He put it down again. He studied Barney's face, but it was without guile.

Tracy said, "Some call it radio, Barney. Who told you that?"

Barney shook his head. "One of the boys. I won't tell you which. You sing, or what?"

"I write. *Millie's Millions.*"

"Is that a program?"

"It's been called worse. Ask your wife about it; she'll tell you."

"I ain't married."

"Then get married, and ask your wife about it. Here's mud in your eye."

Another customer—a stranger—came in, and Barney wandered off. Tracy picked up the fourth paper. There was a headline over a two-column story in a bottom corner of the first page that read:

JEWELER SLAIN
IN HOTEL ROOM

That *might* be it. That *was* it. Tracy caught a glimpse of the name of the jeweler near the top of the minion type. He took a deep breath and read the article carefully.

One Walther Mueller, a wholesale jeweler, just arrived in New York from Rio de Janeiro, Brazil, had been murdered and robbed in his room at the Jarvis Hotel on Sixth Avenue. He had just disembarked from the Bermuda Clipper plane at La Guardia Field, and had taken a cab from the airport to the hotel. He had been in his room less than an hour when the crime occurred; it was discovered an hour and a half after he had checked in, and apparently he had been dead about an hour.

Tracy looked back to see what edition he was reading and calculated that the discovery had been made only half an hour or so before deadline for that edition. That accounted for the paucity of detail, and undoubtedly the next day's paper would have more about it.

It did. The story was buried back on the sixth page this time, because nothing new had happened, but additional details, such as they were, were there.

Mueller was a Belgian by birth, but a citizen of Brazil. He had been in Rio de Janeiro for many years—since 1928—and had been in business for himself as a jeweler for the last ten years. A week before, he had finished the task of closing out his business there. It was his intention to retire, and he had come to the United States for that purpose—on a visitor's visa, but with the expressed intention of acquiring citizenship here if the authorities would grant it.

He had sold his stock before leaving Brazil, except for one necklace of matched pearls which was in the hands of the customs officers awaiting appraisal, and a few items of personal jewelry. The latter, known (from the customs report) to have included a watch valued at two hundred dollars and a half-carat diamond ring valued at three hundred, had been taken by the murderer. Whatever money had been contained in his wallet was also taken, although a twenty-thousand-dollar bank draft —not negotiable—was not stolen.

From all indications, robbery was the motive. Police believed he had been followed from the airport by someone who knew his identity and—perhaps—knew that he was bringing the matched pearl necklace with him to sell in this country. It was valued at approximately fifteen thousand dollars, a worth-while haul for any jewel thief.

The cause of death had been a blunt instrument, probably a blackjack. Police believed the killer had obtained access to Mueller's hotel room under a pretext—possibly the pretense of being an employee of the hotel—and had struck him down.

Police believed also that the murder had been incidental to the robbery and, in fact, had probably been unintentional. The blow had not been hard enough to have killed an ordinary man, but had been fatal to Mueller, who as the result of a previous severe skull fracture was peculiarly susceptible to head injuries.

Police were rounding up known jewel thieves.

Tracy went through the remaining papers for the week and found no further mention of the case. Apparently there had been no further developments—at least, within that length of time.

Tracy put the last of the papers back on the stool beside him and sat scowling at his reflection in the mirror back of the bar.

There wasn't any connection that he could see between Walther Mueller and the two murders of the past few days. Why the devil had Bates asked him about it?

Merely because Mueller was a jeweler, and the fact that one of his *Murder Can Be Fun* scripts had concerned a jeweler? If so, it seemed rather farfetched, to Tracy. It had happened over two months ago, for one thing, and to a complete stranger—and a foreigner at that. And the method—he couldn't be too sure, because he had written that script some time ago, but he thought his jeweler victim had been shot, not bludgeoned.

No, definitely, he couldn't buy it.

The murders of Dineen and Frank had certain things in common that this murder of a jeweler lacked. First, they were both apparently motiveless crimes, whereas motive was glaringly obvious in the case of Mueller. Second, Frank and Dineen had been known to Tracy; Mueller hadn't. Third, there was no such coincidence of method as the Santa Claus suit or the stuffing of a body into a cold furnace.

Those murders had been—in part at least—actual enactments of his scripts. Put together with the other factors involved in each case, they were past coincidence.

But the murder of a jeweler over two months ago—that wasn't even close enough to *be* a coincidence. Lots of jewelers must be killed from time to time in a city the size of New York.

Yes, Bates had merely checked back to the last death by violence of a jeweler and then had thrown the name at Tracy to see if there would be a reaction.

So forget it, Tracy thought. He'd wasted too much time on it already.

"Barney," he yelled, "what's holding up our drinks?"

Nothing, it developed, was holding up the drinks.

But three shots later, Beckman had not shown up. Nor had any of the boys from the editorial department of the *Blade*. Tracy moved on.

It was still raining. The hell with the rain, he decided, and he walked. He knew, now, where he wanted to go.

Stanislaus—Stan, by the sign over the bar—was alone when Tracy entered. He said, "Mister Tracy!" and grinned, and his face got red at the same time. "Golly, I'm glad you came in. I was going to look you up the first evening off I had. I even thought about closing up this joint tonight to look you up. I owe you a hell of an apology."

"That's all right," Tracy said. "When I figure back what I said, and what you must have thought, I wonder you didn't do worse."

Stan Hrdlicka shook his head. "I didn't have time to do worse. That copper, he come running in the minute I—I don't like to think what I mighta done if he hadn't."

Tracy said, "Let's skip it, Stan. Look, I want to talk about—"

Stan said, "Wait." He came around the end of the bar and went to the front door. He locked it and pulled down the shades. He turned out the lights at the front of the tavern.

He said, "Rainy night; there won't be any business anyway. Let's sit down at the table there and—what you drinking? Me, I like slivovitz. Rather have Scotch?"

"Slivovitz it is," Tracy said. He sat down. Stan brought bottle and glasses and sat across from him. The glasses were tumblers. Stan filled them.

"First," he said, "to Frank, Mr. Tracy." Tracy had to stop at less than half, but Stan tossed off the tumbler of potent brandy as though it were beer. He refilled his glass and brought Tracy's up to the brim again.

He leaned forward. "Frank had told me about you, Mr. Tracy. He said you were the only really good guy in the building, the only friend he had there. He said the others were stuffed shirts. So now I know who you are, you didn't kill Frank. Frank wouldn't make a mistake like that. Frank was smart."

Tracy nodded.

"Me, I'm not," Stan said. "I'm just a lug. Frank was strong in the head. Me, I'm strong in the shoulders and arms. But I'm smart enough to know what I'll do if I find who put a shiv in Frank. I won't use no shiv. I'll take him apart with my bare hands."

He held them out; Tracy looked at them, and didn't doubt it.

Tracy said, "I know how you feel, Stan, but that wouldn't be smart. Let the police handle him."

97

Stan said, "—— the police."

He put his hands flat on the table. He said, "Look, I've read the papers. I know about those radio stories you wrote. But how would that make sense with Frank being killed?"

"I don't know, Stan."

"Look, then. Pretend I didn't read them. Tell me the whole thing and let me ask questions. It's mixed up. Maybe we can straighten it out, huh?"

Tracy was willing. It took an hour, and they were on the second bottle of slivovitz when he finished.

Stan nodded his head slowly for a while when his last question had been answered.

Tracy asked, "Do you know who the little blonde girl Frank spoke of could be?"

"No, and he must have met her recently, Tracy, or he would have told me. Told me about it, I mean, even if he might not have told me who she was. I hadn't seen him for two weeks, about. Falling for a girl—it could be quick, with Frank. He was that kind of a guy—uh—what you call it?"

"Romantic?"

"That's it. Romantic. The kind that would fall hard and sudden when he did fall. I don't mean he was a—a monk. He'd had affairs, but they didn't mean anything. I think he was having one, or had had one, with some woman in that building, the Smith Arms."

"The hell," said Tracy. "Who?"

"I don't know. I just know from what he said it wasn't serious; I mean he wasn't in love with her. It was just—well, a guy is human. You know what I mean."

Tracy said, "I know what you mean. Was she married?"

"I—I don't know. I think so. When I first heard Frank was murdered, that is what I thought first. The husband found them together, or found out.

"It'd be so simple if that was it. I mean, it was the only motive, the only reason. People kill for money or for love, and Frank didn't have money. But then comes this business of the other murder, and both of them going by the stories you wrote. It makes nuts, Tracy."

Gloomily he emptied the last of the second slivovitz bottle into their glasses. The hand that did the pouring was steady, and Tracy looked at it wonderingly. At them, really, for he saw two hands and two bottles.

Tracy was drunk. Suddenly and soddenly. The room was swaying and seemed to be part of a vast merry-go-round that went a half circle in one direction and then a half circle in the other.

He saw Stan's face, doubled, looking at him queerly, the same concerned expression on his face. He tried to focus his eyes to bring them together into one image, and couldn't.

It wasn't a new experience, but never before had it hit him so hard and so suddenly. Dimly he realized that never before had he drunk most of a fifth of slivovitz on top of a few whiskies on a completely empty stomach. He'd forgotten all about eating.

It came to him that he'd better stand up, and quickly.

It had come to him wrong. It was definitely a mistake. Sitting down, he might have been all right, for a while at least. But when he stood up, the floor tilted treacherously and he started to fall forward. That was his last conscious memory, starting to fall. If he landed, he never knew it; if Stan managed to catch him, he never knew that either.

CHAPTER 9

THEY SHOULDN'T have happened to a dog, those dreams. They didn't; they happened to Tracy.

The pink cloud, with a very blonde and very dimpled and very décolleté Dotty enshrined upon it, and Tracy trying to climb up to her and the little green devil pushing him back with a very sharp overgrown salad fork, screaming, "Not without the General's permission. Not without the General's permission."

And, in the way of dreams, Tracy's mind asking the question without his lips saying it, and the imp shouting, "Motors, you fool, General Motors. You've got to get the General's permission to get on this program, for he's the sponsor, and you can't be a professional."

"A professional what?" Tracy wondered, and the imp yelled, "A professional anything. This is an amateur hour and you can't get up there if you're a professional." And he jerked a thumb at the décolleté Dotty behind him. "Know what *she* is? This is an amateur hour, and she's an *amateur houri!*"

And the little green devil must have dropped the fork, for there he was holding up a big placard that read LAUGHTER—only Tracy didn't laugh. The pink cloud gave way and he fell into it, horse and all, with another voice calling "Hi-yo Silver, away," in the darkness that was inside the cloud, and there was the clopping of hoofs and shooting, and there Tracy, in undershirt and shorts, was standing in front of Wilkins' desk with Wilkins glaring at him through the pince-nez glasses and saying, "Milliemilliemilliemillie."

Tracy ducked quickly, before Wilkins could see how he was dressed, or wasn't, and stuck his head up past the edge of the desk, watching Wilkins' face get yellower and yellower until it was just the shade of the yellow copy paper that was stacked up on Tracy's desk, and getting blanker and squarer until it *was* a blank sheet of yellow copy paper with "Milliemilliemilliemillie" typed on it, that and nothing else.

But Wilkins' voice was talking out of the sheet of yellow paper, saying, "You understand, Mr. Tracy, that we cannot have the remotest suggestion of suggestiveness on a—ah—program that is sent into every American Home. You must remember to Keep It Clean, Mr. Tracy, like the great soap powder it advertises, children cry for it, so why not you?"

Only as he talked, the blank piece (except for the typed line "Milliemilliemilliemillie") of yellow paper that had been Wilkins' face was changing again, into a red-cheeked face with a long white beard. It was a Santa Claus face or mask now, but wearing gold-rimmed pince-nez glasses, and there was a red cap above the mask and a red flannel suit below it, and it was snowing in the office, and very cold for August, with Tracy shivering there in his underwear and saying, "Yes, Mr. Wilkins," whenever Wilkins paused.

Then Wilkins reached up and took off the mask, and under it wasn't Wilkins' prim little face at all, but the sharp-eyed ferret face of Inspector Bates. And Bates said, "There is a gun pointing at you under the desk, Tracy. It was pointing at you while you were talking to her. *Or were you?*"

Bates smiled that wintry smile of his, then, with the snow swirling down around him, and his eyes got steely again as he said, "A two-move problem, Tracy. Look it over—out the window, there."

So without walking across at all, Tracy was standing at the window looking down into the KRBY inner courtyard, and the courtyard was a chessboard with monstrous black and white chessmen that were grotesque caricatures of most of the people he knew. The white ones were, anyway. He could recognize Jerry Evers and Millie Wheeler and Mr. Wilkins and Mrs. Murdock. And Helen Armstrong and Dick Kreburn and Dotty and Pete Meyer.

"White to move and mate in two," Bates said.

"But the *black* pieces," Tracy wanted to know, "who are the *black?*"

Bates was laughing, laughing like hell, and the laughter growing higher and higher in pitch, with an echo-chamber effect, and he said, "You should know. You wrote them—black on yellow paper!" And his voice kept getting higher and higher until it was the buzz of a sawmill, and Tracy was tied down to the car that was carrying him into the huge spinning saw, along the tracks. It was zipping now through the big log on the car ahead, and Tracy was next, stark naked and tied down hand and foot. He tried to yell and couldn't. He managed to lift his head. There was a placard on the end of the log ahead of him. It read in big red letters APPLAUSE; then the saw buzzed through the placard and was coming in between Tracy's feet.

He tried again to yell, and couldn't. But he woke up.

He woke to darkness and the buzzing of a saw, and he could move, but he didn't try after that first convulsive jerk away from the saw, on awakening. It nearly took the top off his head —the jerk, not the saw. The saw was someone snoring. Tracy reached out on both sides of him, but he was alone in the bed.

Outside somewhere a clock struck half past something. Tracy sat up in bed, slowly and carefully, and put his feet out over the side. His feet were bare. His hands, investigating, told him he was stripped down to shorts and undershirt.

The cool smoothness of linoleum under his bare feet proved to him what he had already felt pretty sure of; he wasn't in his own room.

The inside of his mouth felt like dry, cracked leather. The only important thing in the world was a drink of cold water—a gallon or two of cold water.

A bit to his left and about six feet away he saw a thin yellow line that looked like the crack under a door leading to a lighted room. With infinite care, he stood up and made his way toward it, groping ahead of him and placing each foot carefully. He got to the door, found the knob, and opened it.

Outside the door was a dingy hallway with peeling wallpaper of a bilious green. He stuck his head through the opening cautiously and looked around. There was a flight of stairs going up and another flight going down. There were other closed doors off the hallway and there was one door, painted white a long time ago, that was ajar. That would be the bathroom.

He opened the door wider and turned around to look over the room in which he had just awakened, in the light that came from the dim hallway. It was a rooming-house bedroom. Besides the bed on which he had awakened, there was a bureau, a table, a few chairs, and a sofa. Asleep on the sofa and snoring like the buzz saw of Tracy's dream was Stan Hrdlicka.

Tracy left the door ajar and went down the hall to the bathroom. He drank several glasses of water, and came back. He found that Stan had rolled over and wasn't snoring any more.

He closed the door softly and groped back to the bed. He sat down on the edge of it and felt like hell for a while. He wondered if he should hunt for his clothes and go home. He didn't wonder long; he decided the hell with it.

He lay back down and was asleep again almost before he could close his eyes.

He woke again later and found himsel covered with cold sweat. He groped at the foot of his bed and found a sheet, which he pulled up over him. This time it was harder for him to go back to sleep. Slivovitz, he thought; the last time I ever drink slivovitz.

I'm a mess, he thought. A ghastly mess. I've got to cut out drinking so much. Especially on an empty stomach. Man does not live on drink alone. Not and write radio continuity. Millie —what the hell could happen to Millie Mereton next? He *had* to have a new sequence for her soon, or he'd be out of a job. Burned out. Or maybe drowned out.

Mrs. Murdock—could he run in a character like her? But how could she fit into the plot? And—no, Wilkins wouldn't like it. She was too much like too many women who listened to the program. He couldn't satirize his audience.

What a mess, that business in the cellar. Inspector Bates standing there with a gun pointed at him. Just in case he really *was* a homicidal maniac who acted out his own scripts. Bates could believe that was possible.

Nuts to Bates. Bates wasn't getting anywhere at all. His smartest deduction to date was that it must have been a man who killed Frank, because it would take a man's strength to stuff the body into the furnace.

But *would* it? Not if the woman was Mrs. Murdock. She looked as strong as a horse. What if Frank (God forbid) had been having an affair with *her?* And then broken it off when he'd seen or met the little blonde he wanted to marry someday.

A woman like that might kill him. A woman like that might do anything. But how would she have known about the janitor-in-the-furnace script?

Wait, he thought, that wasn't impossible. Frank had a key to his apartment. Frank *could* have read those scripts himself and talked about them to his paramour.

103

It got him wide awake for a moment, that startling possibility. But then he thought of the ridiculousness of Mrs. Murdock's having donned a Santa suit and gone gunning for Arthur Dineen.

He turned over and tried to go back to sleep. And this time he succeeded, but he didn't lose the idea of Mrs. Murdock maybe having killed Frank. That was in the background of his dream, but his dream was about *Mr.* Murdock, who turned out to be seven feet tall and to have bright red hair and buck teeth. It was Mr. Murdock, he dreamed, who had killed Dineen because Dineen wouldn't buy an insurance policy.

It wasn't a mixed-up dream like the first one; it seemed to make cold sense that it had really happened that way. It got out of hand only when Mr. Murdock, fleeing the police, kidnaped Millie Mereton to hold her as hostage. That, of course, solved the next sequence of *Millie's Millions,* but with Millie kidnaped too soon, she hadn't raised the money for her brother, Reggie, to put back in the bank, and the examiners caught him and put him in jail. Only it was Dick Kreburn who was in jail, rather than the character he played on the air, and it was Millie Wheeler—the real Millie—who was helping Tracy try to get him out before he caught laryngitis again from a damp cell.

At gray dawn, Tracy wakened once more and again drank a lot of water. After that, he slept dreamlessly, and long.

It was broad daylight when Stan shook him awake. Stan was dressed and grinning down at him. He said, "Eleven o'clock, Mr. Tracy. Just twelve hours since I tucked you in."

Tracy sat up. He looked at the clock on the bureau and groaned. He should have been at the studio long ago.

"Where are we?" he asked.

Stan said, "Upstairs over the tavern. I room in the same building. You went out like a light, so I just brought you up here. Look, I got to leave; that's why I waked you. Take your time about getting dressed and going. I guess you can find your way out all right."

Tracy nodded. He said, "Thanks a lot, Stan. My God, I never did *that* before. Hadn't eaten all day; guess that was why."

When Stan had left, Tracy ran his hand over his face to see how badly he needed a shave. Then he looked at the clock again and decided the hell with it. If he hurried, he'd still not get to the studio until noon or later. And he'd look like the devil when he got there. Better forget it entirely; after all, today's script was patched up okay.

He took his time dressing, and went to the Smith Arms.

He was putting the key into the lock of his door when Millie's door flew open.

"Tracy!" she said. "Thank God. I was worried about you. What happened? I mean—it isn't my business if you—I mean—"

Tracy grinned at her. "Not that at all, angel. I spent the night with Frank Hrdlicka's brother. We—uh—talked so late, I decided to stay with him when he suggested it."

"Frank's brother, the bartender?"

Tracy looked surprised. "You know him?"

"No. Sergeant Corey mentioned him. That's how I knew you didn't come home last night. I mean, the sergeant was here early this morning looking for you. When you didn't answer, he asked if I knew where you were. Then he got the passkey and let himself in, and came over to tell me that your bed hadn't been slept in at all."

"Oh," said Tracy. "Was he going to notify the police?"

"Don't be silly. But he said he'd be back at two in the afternoon and if you weren't here then, or hadn't shown up at the studio or anywhere, they'd start looking for you. Had breakfast, Tracy?"

"No, but I need a bath and a shave first. But—you must have had breakfast, if you were up early."

"Sure. I was just going to start some lunch for myself. You can call it breakfast. Twenty minutes?"

"Twenty-one," said Tracy.

It took him twenty-five, but he felt human again. He'd thought he would want only coffee, but was surprised to find himself ravenous. He ate twice as much as Millie did. It was one-thirty when they finished, and Millie had to leave for a posing appointment.

Tracy went back to his own place to wait for Corey to show up. While he waited, he phoned the studio and asked for Dotty.

"Tracy," he said, when he heard her voice. "Was his nibs mad that I didn't get there this morning?"

"I think he was, a little," she said. "His secretary told me he'd had her phone you several times, and you weren't home."

"Wasn't I?" Tracy managed to sound surprised. "How did today's program go?"

"All right, I guess. Oh, Dick Kreburn was in. His sore throat's a lot better. He could have gone on today, but Mr. Wilkins said that since we'd already written him out of the script to let it stand. But he can go back on the air tomorrow, as long as we keep it in the script that he's still a little hoarse."

"Swell," Tracy said. He felt a few of the cares of the world slipping from his shoulders. "And now about tonight. When and where shall I pick you up and where shall we eat, and what shall I buy tickets for?"

"Oh, let's not go anywhere, Mr. Tracy. You were going to tell me about radio writing, weren't you? I *do* want you to help me. Let's eat at my place."

"Don't tell me you can *cook*, too, Dotty!"

"Not too badly. Is that all right with you?"

"It's marvelous. What can I bring besides my own sweet self?"

"I have everything. Unless you maybe you want to bring a bottle of wine. Whatever kind you like, if you like wine, I mean."

Tracy said, "I'll bring a jug of it. A loaf of bread, a jug of wine, and thou beside me singing in the wil—By the way, where *is* the wilderness?"

Dotty giggled a little, and gave him the address. It was in the Village. And, in case he was detained or forced to change plans, she suggested he take the phone number as well.

After the receiver was back on the hook, Tracy sat for a moment smiling fatuously at the telephone. A marvelous invention, the telephone. A marvelous girl, Dotty—Dotty what? For the first time it occurred to him that he didn't know her last name. Well, unless the phone was an unlisted one, he could find out easily without the embarrassment of asking anyone.

Through Information, he got the exchange clerk and asked for the listing. "One moment, please," said a sweet voice, and a moment and a half later, "The telephone is listed in the name of Miss Dorothea Mueller, Apartment Seven, Two-fourteen Waverly Place."

"Miss Dorothea *what?*"

"Muller," said the sweet voice, and with sweet reasonableness spelled it out for him. "M-u-e-l-l-e-r."

This time, Tracy sat staring at the phone, but without the fatuous smile.

It was just a coincidence. It *had* to be a coincidence. How many people in New York were named Mueller? Millions of them. And this Walther Mueller hadn't even been a New Yorker. He was a Belgian from Brazil, come to New York to retire. Or at any rate, to the United States to retire; he probably hadn't planned to stay in New York at all.

What possible connection could he have with a blonde stenographer who wrote love pulp stories? The newspapers hadn't mentioned any relatives. True, they hadn't said he didn't have any.

But—there was that damn chill down his spine again, that prickling sensation on his scalp. There'd been too damn many coincidences in this business.

Or had there? They'd decided that the two murders had *not* been coincidences, hadn't they? They'd been too close for that. But a mere coincidence of a fairly common name—surely that could be a genuine one, couldn't it? Of course it could. Nuts to it, then; forget it.

He wouldn't even be silly enough to ask Dotty about it.

He took a deep breath, and felt better.

The doorbell rang, and he went to let Sergeant Corey in. It was just exactly two o'clock.

Corey grinned his way across the room and into the chair.

He said, "How'd you like it?" and the grin got wider. Tracy watched suspiciously, but the sergeant didn't vanish and leave the grin suspended in mid-air.

"Like what?" Tracy asked.

"The story. The publicity I got you. Made front page in every paper. Bates wasn't going to give it out, but I talked him into it. Wasn't it a dilly of a story, huh?"

"Well—"

"I knew you really wanted it in the papers. Hell, it was a *natural* for publicity for a writer."

The sergeant was in a jovial mood. He laughed out loud. He said, "Know what Bates thinks?"

"Yeah," said Tracy. "He thinks I did it."

Corey slapped his knee. "That's right. Both of them. And that jeweler guy, too, maybe. He's nuts. My wife, even, says he's nuts, and she hasn't even met you—just knows what I told her about you and what program you write.

"Say, you know she wasn't mad at all about my getting home drunk the other night. Says if I was with the guy writes *Millie's Millions,* I couldn't go wrong. Says if a guy could write stuff like that—well, he couldn't *be* a wrong guy, if you know what I mean."

Tracy lifted an eyebrow. He asked, "And what does Bates think of that line of reasoning?"

Corey chuckled. "He looks at it the other way. He listened in to a program the other day, and he says a guy who'd write that crap would do anything. Hell, you can't please everybody, I guess."

"Drink?" Tracy asked.

"I'm on dut—Hell, sure I'll have a drink."

Tracy got the bottle from the kitchenette. He poured two making his own a short one.

"To crime," Corey said. "Say, that gal across the hall. Millie. She was plenty worried you didn't get home last night. She must like you a lot. Now me, if I had a gal like that feeling that way about me, I wouldn't be lapping up slivovitz with no mug. And didn't you kind of take a chance, Mr. Tracy?"

"On what?"

"On that Stan. Hell, he could take you—or me—apart in little pieces. And if he ever got the idea again that you killed his brother, we'll know where to look for you. Matter of fact, that was where I did look. Didn't tell Miss Wheeler, though; I didn't want to worry her."

"You saw Stan, today?"

"Sure. Got there just after you left, and he told me about it. He could be bad medicine, Tracy, if he got the wrong idea again."

"But he knows better now."

"Sure, Mr. Tracy; when he's sober. But when a guy like that gets drunk, he can get all kinds of funny ideas again. Drinking with him, like you did, is like playing with TNT. So from Stan's I went around to the studio, and just come here from there."

"See Wilkins?"

Corey shook his head. "Not many of 'em there. Most of 'em were going to the funeral—the Dineen funeral."

Tracy snapped his fingers. He said, "Damn, I had a hunch I was forgetting something. I was going to—" He looked around at the clock. "Well, it's too late to start now."

"Bates went out there. Say, what do you know about this Jerry Evers from the studio?"

"Not a lot. Nice guy."

Corey frowned. "Acted suspicious as hell, when Bates and I talked to him. Can't remember where he was when anything happened, and admitted he hated Dineen. Acted scared stiff, too."

"Does Bates suspect him?"

"Naw, Bates thinks he was just acting up. Maybe looking for some free publicity by trying to get himself pinched. But me—I don't know. It could've been him, easy as anybody else. Only guy we've come across had a grudge against both Dineen *and* Hrdlicka."

"Huh? He hardly knew Frank."

Corey shook his head. "Told us he'd played cards with him

and you. And that there'd been an argument about cheating. Says we'd find out anyway, so he might as well tell us."

Tracy laughed. "That was just a joke. They were kidding each other about cards up their sleeves. Pinochle, at a nickel a hand."

"Some guys don't kid about stuff like that. You can't be sure. Well, look, what I really came about was just to check up if you had anything new."

"Not a thing, Sarge."

"Then I guess I'll mosey along. Be seeing you around. And listen—be careful what you say to Stan, if you see him again. Ever occur to you he may have got you drunk last night on purpose to see if you'd talk too much? In your sleep, if not before?"

"Did he say that?"

"Well, no. But we got talking, and he mentioned you *did* do some talking in your sleep. Something about some dame named Dotty. Nothing—uh—coherent."

Tracy laughed. "There's nothing coherent to talk about, yet. Have a stirrup cup, Sarge?"

"Huh? Oh, you mean a drink. Guess one more won't hurt me."

Apparently it didn't. He departed unharmed.

Tracy stood looking at the door a moment after he had closed it. Then he went over to the Morris chair and sat there trying to think.

Why in hell had Sergeant Corey gone out of his way to tell Tracy that Inspector Bates still suspected him? Was it Corey's idea, or Bates'? In either case, why?

There were, Tracy thought, three definite possibilities. One was that Corey was actually as stupid as he seemed, and completely on the up-and-up; that he was being friendly and nothing more.

Second, he might be a little cleverer than that, being Machiavellian in an Airedale sort of way. Probably in collusion with Inspector Bates. To what end, only God knew.

Third, it was just possible that he was smarter yet. Smart

enough deliberately to act too stupid to seem possible. A sort of reverse English. To what end, in that case, maybe even God didn't know.

It was a fascinating problem. After considerable thought, Tracy decided the second idea was best. He couldn't see how a man as dumb as Corey had just pretended to be could have obtained stripes in the homicide department, for one thing. And as for being a mental superman—that wouldn't sit right, either.

It was elephantine subtlety, then. But *why?*

He gave it up, had another very short drink, and put the bottle firmly away. He had to be sober for this evening.

And sober he was when, laden with wine and hope, he entered the building at Two-fourteen Waverly Place. He glanced along the mailboxes. Yes, Dorothea Mueller, Apartment Seven.

Mueller—*damn* the name. Should he ask—? Hell, no, he thought, why risk spoiling an evening? If she did turn out to have a connection with a man named Walther Mueller, to be his daughter or something, then—

No, don't ask. Because it wouldn't simplify anything if he got the wrong answer; it would complicate it beyond endurance.

The latch of the inner door clicked in response to his ringing of the bell and he went in and up the stairs to the second floor.

CHAPTER 10

DOTTY, LOOKING delightfully domestic in a green print frock, smiled at him from the doorway of the front apartment.

"Hungry?" she asked, taking the wine from him and carrying it toward the kitchenette. "Or shall we talk a while first before we eat?"

He told her he wasn't hungry, and went walking after her toward the kitchenette, but she sent him firmly back and told him to sit down, that she'd open and pour the wine.

Tracy sat hopefully on the sofa, but when Dotty came back with two glasses of the wine, she took the armchair.

"Mr. Tracy—"

"Bill, to you."

"Bill, I've got *so* many questions I want to ask you about radio writing. You do it so marvelously. If I could only—"

Better men have fallen for harder soap. He found himself telling her the tricks of the trade, the little ones that make big differences. Things like: ". . . and another thing to watch out for, Dotty. When an actor is supposed to be there, he's got to say something every few lines, or he 'dies,' as a radio writer would call it. People just forget he's there, because they can't see him. If there are three people in a scene, for instance, you can't have a conversation just between two of them—the third one has got to chip in frequently even if he only says 'Yes' or 'Huh?' or something like that. Ten speeches, with him left out, and he's faded out of the listeners' memory—and it's a comic effect if he suddenly pops out with something. In fact, it's an effect that's used deliberately on some of the comic shows. . . ."

And then dinner, and it turned out that Dotty really could cook. Competently, if not superbly. It was a casserole dish with shrimp, and definitely it was good enough to eat.

Helping Dotty with the dishes—over her protest—was very companionable and cozy, but the talk was still radio. If and when it digressed, Dotty brought it back.

And when the dishes were done, Dotty was in the armchair again, and Tracy had the sofa all to himself, as before. But Dotty was so decorative, sitting there, that it was nice just to look at her. And after all, Rome wasn't built in a day, and Dotty was a nice girl.

". . . and about plotting," Tracy was saying. "There's a big difference in plotting soap operas and plotting magazine stories. For a magazine story, you get your characters into a jam and out again, and that's the story. But in radio serials, they've got to get into the next jam before they get out of the last one.

112

And that means you've got to have at least two threads of plot going most of the time."

Dotty sighed prettily. "It's a shame they can't ever be happy, isn't it?"

Tracy said, "Blame that on the audience. People who listen to serials just aren't interested in anyone who's happy."

"I see. So Millie must get into some other kind of trouble before she gets her brother out of his jam at the bank. What sort of sequence are you going to use next, Bill?"

"You *would* bring that up. I haven't thought of one yet. Everything I've thought of has already happened to Millie. Everything I can use on the air, anyway."

"Look, Bill—nothing has happened to Dale Elkins; not for a long time, anyway. Why not have him get hurt in an accident? Get run over by a truck or something. Then you can have hospital scenes and interviews with a doctor who's not sure whether he'll get well or not, and—"

Tracy snapped his fingers.

"Dotty, that's it. You're a wonder-child. And here's the build-up we'll use: Just before he gets run over or whatever, he and Millie quarrel about nothing and she sends him off in a huff. Doesn't mean it, of course, because she really loves him, and it's just a lovers' quarrel.

"So that's what makes it dramatic when he's hurt and unconscious. Her conscience will give her hell for being mean to him. She's even afraid he'll die without coming to, so she can ask him to forgive her. Let's see—the quarrel can be mostly her fault, and she'll realize it after it's too late. And he can be unconscious for a full week's scripts, even if it's only eight or ten hours of elapsed time—"

"Bill, wasn't there a doctor once who was in love with Millie? A year or so ago?"

Tracy nodded. "One of the parts Jerry Evers played. Ummm —he used a pretty distinctive tone of voice for it, I believe. I think he could come back in that role without interfering with the role he's handling now—the head teller at the bank."

"Bill, he could be put in charge of the case when Dale is brought into the hospital, couldn't he?"

Tracy nodded slowly. "Ashes of an old love, and the blood of the new one. Dotty, you're marvelous. Or did I tell you that?"

They talked until a little after midnight, and then Tracy found himself being eased gently out into the night. Gently, but so definitely that the good-night kiss he gave her was chaste and deceptively unambitious.

But it tingled on his lips while he walked home.

Yes, a nice girl, Dotty. And that was a nice little apartment she had, and a swell meal she'd given him, and a swell idea for the next Millie sequence. Dammit, that idea was worth money to him; he ought to give her a cut out of his income while that sequence ran. But of course she wouldn't take it. He'd have to make it up to her in other ways.

Maybe he and Dotty could collaborate on a brand-new soap opera idea, get it on sustaining through KRBY, get a sponsor. . . .

It wasn't until he was almost home that it occurred to him to wonder how, on a stenographer's salary, Dotty could afford an apartment like that. If he knew anything about Village rentals, that place cost almost as much as a stenographer's entire salary at the studio. And Dotty dressed well, too, for a stenographer.

It took him a minute to get the answer, and then he was surprised at how simple it was. The love pulp magazine stories, of course. Probably that was her main source of income, and she was working at the studio just to get radio experience so she could crash the soapy gates.

At home, Tracy put Dotty resolutely out of mind—or at any rate, out of the center of his mind—and sat down at the typewriter desk. While it was fresh, he should dash off a synopsis of the new sequence so he could take it in to Wilkins tomorrow morning for an okay. Let's see, tomorrow was Saturday and there'd be no Millie show, but Wilkins would be there until noon, anyway.

He yanked paper into the Underwood and clicked out the heading.

Then he lighted a cigarette and stared at the keyboard. What would Millie and Dale quarrel about?

Half an hour later, he was still sitting there staring at the keys. He knew intimately, now, that the top row of them, under the figure row, read QWERTYUIOP¼ and that the middle row read ASDFGHJKL:@. But he still hadn't thought of anything reasonable for Millie and Dale to quarrel about. Dammit, they were such wishy-washy characters, both of them, that what *was* there for them to scrap over?

Annoyed, he yanked the paper out of the machine and threw it into the wastebasket. He pulled the cover up over the typewriter so that the damned QWERTYUIOP¼ wouldn't gibber up at him.

He just wasn't in the mood to write, or to think constructively, tonight. He'd get a few hours' sleep, get up early, and it would go like a breeze. Dammit, he had the main idea—and it was just plain silly to let himself be stymied by minor details. He'd do a synopsis tomorrow morning, and if the minor details didn't come, he'd leave them out. After all, he needed only a rough synopsis.

He set the alarm for eight, and turned in.

But he lay there worrying for a while. *Was* he getting burned out as a writer? He'd heard of it happening to people, but it always seemed like something that happened to somebody else. Not to Bill Tracy.

Then his mind went back to Dotty, and soon he slept. And dreamed.

* * *

The strident clangor of the alarm clock wakened him to a futile world. He shut it off, as quickly as he could, and lay there staring at the unresponsive ceiling, thinking what an utter botch he had made of the last few days. He hadn't written a word. He hadn't even had a constructive thought of his own either about *Millie's Millions* or about the murders.

True, he now had the general outline of an idea, but it had been Dotty's, not his. He hadn't even had brains enough to fill in the minor details. Would he have to ask Dotty to do that, too?

And now in the dim light of dawn—well, not dawn exactly, but the light would be dim until he got up and raised the shades —he'd have to get up and sit down at that blankety-blank typewriter and grind *something* out. Either that or have a scene with Wilkins.

He'd never felt less like writing in his life. Dammit, he should have known better than to put it off until morning. He *never* felt up to doing anything creative right after breakfast. And before breakfast, even thinking about it hurt him.

He groaned and tried to forget about *Millie's Millions*. But that took him back to the murders. Silly murders, without rhyme or reason. And were they over? He had a feeling that they weren't.

Who was next?

And rather than try to figure that out—with no basis to figure from—he got out of bed and stumbled to the shower. The cold water didn't fully wake him, but it helped.

Dressed, he decided that he didn't want any breakfast. He'd better get that damn synopsis started. He took the cover off his typewriter and sat down.

Let's see—Dale and Millie had to quarrel, and the first question was what they were to quarrel about. Let's see—

Hell, his mind was still foggy. He'd better go downstairs for some coffee first.

In the hallway, he met Millie Wheeler coming in, with packages.

"Tracy!" she said. "What on earth gets you up at the awful hour of eight-thirty? Or haven't you been to bed yet?"

"My busy day, angel. Got to work. *Really* work."

"Had breakfast?"

"Going out for coffee now. Come along?"

"Here's coffee." She handed him a package. And the others. "Take the rest of it, so I can get the door open."

He followed her in, put the packages in the kitchenette, and sat down. She started the coffee.

"What's doing, Tracy? *Millie's Millions* scripts?"

"Synopsis for the next sequence. Millie's going to quarrel with Dale, and then he goes out and gets hit by a truck."

"Good idea. I mean, Dale getting hit by a truck. What are they going to quarrel about?"

"That hasn't cooked yet. Got any suggestions?"

"Ummm," said Millie, "let me think a minute." She brought plates and cups from the kitchenette and set them on the table. "Why not have Millie find out Dale's making passes at a blonde?"

"Say, that's swe—"

Sudden suspicion hit Tracy, but he couldn't verify it. Millie was bending over the stove to break eggs into the little pyrex skillet and he couldn't see her face.

"—swell," he said. "Uh—go on with it. Where does he meet the blonde?"

"Well, he works at an office, doesn't he? Why not have her work there. A new stenographer, maybe."

"Yeah," said Tracy. Since her back was still toward him anyway, he let his eyes narrow into a look of dark suspicion. "And then what happens?"

"He gets hit by a truck," said Millie cheerfully. "That's what you said. And it serves him right, doesn't it? How many lumps?"

"Where? In my coffee?"

"Certainly, you dope." She turned around, and her face was without guile.

Tracy insisted on helping her with the dishes after breakfast. Maybe it was his conscience. Then he was shooed out so she could dress to go to the studio.

He wandered disconsolately back to the typewriter in his own apartment. Resolutely he put in white paper, carbon, and yellow second sheet.

Resolutely he typed a heading, turned the roller down, and

started to type out the synopsis. Had Millie's suggestion been a shot in the dark? Or—?

Well, it was a workable idea, anyhow. Only he compromised by making the girl a comptometer operator instead of a stenographer, and a redhead instead of a blonde. At least *that* much of the synopsis, he thought bitterly, would be his own idea and not Dotty's or Millie's. And, of course, Dale wouldn't really be guilty of attempted philandering (Wilkins would thumb that down, anyway) but would be a victim of misleading appearances.

He kept on going; it came out slowly, a word at a time. Each word hurt. The synopsis was a brief one, two pages double-spaced, and it took him until eleven o'clock to finish it.

There was sweat on his forehead, and it wasn't all from the August heat. That had been the toughest piece of writing he'd ever done—even though he'd sat down with the idea ready to write. And not even his own—Of course! That was why it had been so hard, *because* it hadn't been his own.

He sighed with relief at the comforting thought, and got out quickly. He'd have to hurry to be sure of catching Wilkins. And Wilkins was probably fuming. It was a wonder he hadn't called on the phone.

But the ordeal turned out to be not too bad.

Wilkins frowned when Tracy entered his office, but thawed out when the synopsis was on the desk before him. He read it slowly and nodded. "It'll do," he said. "Any of the continuity ready?"

"Thought I'd get your approval on the synopsis first, in case you want to suggest any changes. I can have a few scripts by Monday."

"Fine. I might suggest one slight change. Wouldn't it seem more—ah—usual to have the girl at the office a blonde? I mean—"

"No," said Tracy. "For that very reason, *not* a blonde. A brunette, if you think a redhead would be too *outré*."

Wilkins' right eyebrow went up a trifle. "You don't—ah—care for blondes, Mr. Tracy? Somehow I got the impression—"

Tracy grinned. "It's not personal, Mr. Wilkins. Just the fact that blondes have been overworked for that sort of thing. They're hackneyed. But speaking of blondes, is Dotty around? With a stenographer, I might get a start at those scripts now, in one of the offices."

"She has probably left. She works only until noon on Saturday and it's now—yes, it's ten minutes after. Miss Hill is working this afternoon, I believe. Shall I have her type for you?"

"Never mind, Mr. Wilkins. I can work better, really, by myself. I just thought that it would—sort of help Dotty on the radio writing angle, if she were working anyway."

"I see. It's unfortunate, then, that she's gone. By the way, Mr. Tracy, there is one point in this sequence that is definitely debatable. I mean, the possibility which you suggest of Dale Elkins actually dying. That is a major point which would have to be taken up with our sponsors. We could not take any such —ah—radical step without their approval."

"Of course," Tracy said. "That's why I merely suggested it as a possibility. The business of the quarrel will take several days—the same several in which we're finally extricating Reggie from his difficulty at the bank. Then, just before the last script that will concern the bank angle, will come the accident. And all the hospital scenes—they're good for weeks."

Wilkins nodded. "I'm seeing our sponsor Tuesday. I'll show him this synopsis and get his opinion. But I'll guarantee that the first part—the quarrel and the accident and the early hospital scenes—will be satisfactory. You may go ahead with a week's scripts, even two weeks', on that basis."

Tracy felt better as he took the elevator down. One hurdle had been taken. Now if he could get a couple of scripts done over Sunday—

Force of habit rather than serious desire for drink turned his steps toward the bar downstairs. He ordered a bottle of beer and nursed it along, getting up courage to go home and tackle the scripts. He had a hunch it would be tough going.

Why in hell did there have to be scripts due *now?* Why

hadn't he been further ahead of the game when this murder business came up? If there was only some way he could take a vacation for a week and forget all about *Millie's Millions*—

A bulky figure moved in beside him at the bar.

"Hi, Tracy," said Sergeant Corey's voice. "I was just upstairs to see if you was there, and Mr. Wilkins told me you'd probably drop in here on your way out."

"A smart cookie, that Wilkins," said Tracy. "What'll you have, Sarge?"

"Well—guess a beer won't hurt me. But don't tell the Inspector. Just happened to be near here and thought I'd tell you something we found out, if you were around. We found out where the Santa Claus suit came from."

Tracy put down his beer. "Where?"

"Seabright's, the theatrical costumer's. They had a burglary last Monday night—the night before Dineen was killed. They'd reported it, but hadn't reported anything stolen. Didn't come to our department, naturally, and we didn't know about it until this morning."

"When they missed the Santa suit?"

Corey nodded sagely. "Right on the head. Y'see, when they found the place had been broken into, Tuesday morning, they first looked for the cash—there was only a few dollars in a change drawer—and it was all there, so they figured the burglar hadn't found it. They gave the stock a quick once-over, but didn't open every box. But then this morning they got a request for a Santa suit, and they missed it."

"Who the hell would want a Santa suit this time of year?"

"Ah," said the sergeant.

Tracy frowned. "Never met him. Any relation to Lo, the poor Indian? Or wait—I *do* know an Ah. Back in Buffalo. Used to take my shirts to him. Ah Lee Soong, I think his name was."

"You're kidding me, Mr. Tracy."

"Bet you ten. We can get a telephone directory of Buffalo and—Hey, Hank, two bottles of beer. All right, Sarge, I'll bite. Who tried to rent a Santa suit this morning? And I'll sit at your feet with bated breath."

"Jerry Evers, that's who. That character actor that had the fight with Dineen, and the quarrel with Frank Hrdlicka."

"Oh," said Tracy.

"He's down at the bureau now. They're talking to him."

"What's his story?"

"Screwy as hell, but hard to disprove. Said he had a hunch the Santa suit the murderer must have used, well, that it must have been swiped from a costumer, and that he was going the rounds asking for one. Said he thought he might find out something we missed."

Tracy said, "That's not so screwy, is it? He did. I mean he did find something you missed."

"Well—yeah. We did check on the suit angle, naturally, to the extent of phoning all costumers around town to ask if they'd rented or sold any Santa suits recently, and none of 'em had. I guess—well, we should have gone farther and asked them to check their stock to see if any suits was missing, but hell, we didn't think of that. We thought if one had been stolen, they'd say so. Only Seabright's didn't know it was stolen."

"Had Jerry Evers really been to other places asking for a suit?"

"One other, yeah. We checked. He'd asked for a suit and looked at it, and said he wanted one of better material—it was cheap flannel—and he did ask 'em if that was the only one they had and if they'd rented or sold any recently. Seabright's was the second place he went. But of course he'd have gone to more than one place to back up his story."

"Drink your beer before it gets flat, Sarge. So all right—if Jerry is the killer and if he stole that Santa suit Monday night, then what in hell possible reason would he have for calling attention to it being missing by going around and asking for it?"

Corey sipped his beer slowly. He said, "I dunno. But we figure the killer is probably crazy. So he would do something

121

screwy like that. He can't let well enough alone, maybe. He gets a crazy notion he's covering his tracks by bringing out where the suit came from, since we can't prove he did the burgling. Figures he's trying to *di*-vert suspicion."

"And succeeding?"

Corey looked aggrieved. "I told you the guy's crazy. Look, I'll prove it. Suppose he *didn't* kill anybody—this Jerry Evers. Suppose he's pure as the driving snow. All right, then—he didn't like either Dineen or Hrdlicka, so what for is he going out of his way to help find who killed him? He ain't that kind of a guy. He's sneaky and kind of—what's the word I want?— furtive, that's it. Furtive."

Tracy shook his head sadly. Up to a point, at any rate, he wouldn't throw a monkey wrench in Jerry's publicity scheme. But Jerry could go too far. He said, "Hell, Sarge, the guy's an actor."

"Maybe, but I think he's scared stiff. Scared enough to act natural, instead of acting. Well, I got to blow. Just thought I'd tell you the news about the suit. So long."

"So long, Sarge."

Tracy sighed and, after Corey had left, glowered at his reflection in the bar mirror. Damn Jerry Evers, anyway. Looked like he might succeed in getting himself in the papers at that. If he was really charged, he'd get publicity all right. Enough ink to drown him. Then he could conveniently remember his hairdresser alibi and the cops would be holding the bag.

Great stuff, except that while the police were chasing their tails up a blind alley, the real killer could be getting set for another kill. And the real clues, if there were any, were getting freezingly cold.

Damn Jerry Evers.

Tracy finished his second bottle of beer and wandered gloomily out into the midday heat. He tried to think of some good reason for not going home to start those Millie scripts. There wasn't any, except of course that he migh as well eat some lunch first.

Why hadn't he asked Corey to eat with him? He hated the

thought of eating alone when he was going to have to suffer alone all afternoon thereafter. Dammit, why hadn't Dotty worked till one instead of twelve?

Well—maybe Dick Kreburn wouldn't have eaten yet. And he could walk home past Dick's hotel without going too far out of his way.

Dick hadn't eaten. They went for spaghetti to a little Italian place just around the corner from Dick's. Dick's voice was still a trifle hoarse, but he insisted that he could talk as much as he wanted to now.

"The more the better," he said. "My voice'll be normal by Monday."

"Not too normal," Tracy said. "The script calls for you to be hoarse for your Monday and Tuesday parts."

Dick grinned. "That's what I mean. From here on out I *should* talk too much to stay a little hoarse. Maybe I should take singing lessons. Say, how goes the murder business? Haven't had a talk with you since I read about that script business in the papers. Is it the McCoy?"

"The righteous stuff, dammit."

"Look, if there's anything I can do, Tracy—"

"Sure. Find out who the murderer is. No, don't take me seriously. Stay out of it, Dick. The more people get mixed up in it, the worse mixed up the coppers will be. Jerry Evers—"

"Don't tell me Jerry's trying to tangle himself in it, Tracy. I should have guessed. That publicity hound'd murder his grandmother to get an inch on page three."

"He's heading for three columns on page one, with a run-over, damn him." Tracy told what had happened.

Dick shook his head. "You ought to give the guy away, Tracy. Or—maybe not; I don't know. But listen, the police aren't as dumb as you seem to think. Maybe they don't really think he did it; maybe they're using him as a smoke screen to make the real killer confident."

"He *should* be confident," Tracy said. "He should be laughing his head off."

When they had eaten, Tracy manfully resisted temptation to kill the rest of the afternoon with Dick, and went on home.

The typewriter was still there.

He sat down to it and strove mightily. He worked honestly, with the courage of desperation. At six o'clock, after three and three-quarter hours of the toughest labor he'd ever done, he'd got halfway through one script. Even though he'd known *what* he was going to write, the words had come slowly, one at a time. He felt like a dishrag. When he got up to straighten his cramped legs and caught a glimpse of himself in the mirror, he found that he looked like a dishrag, too.

But he grinned at himself in the mirror because he'd just had an idea. A wonderful idea. If only he'd thought of it four hours sooner, he'd have saved himself an afternoon in hell.

Maybe, though, it was just as well he hadn't thought of it then. He felt better now for having proved to himself that he could still put words on paper, at whatever cost.

He picked up the phone and called Dotty.

"Tracy," he said. "Listen, Dotty, I got a proposition to make you. I mean a business proposition, on the level. You free this evening?"

"Why—what I was going to do isn't really important, Bill. I could phone and call it off."

"Do that, then. And have you eaten yet?"

"Why, no."

"Then don't. I'll be right over, soon as I can get there. I'll pick up some grub en route, and we can eat at your place. We can talk better there. 'Bye now."

He took a quick shower to get rid of the dishrag look and then gathered up all the old *Millie's Millions* scripts he could find kicking around, and his carbons of the few that had been written and not yet played. He put them into a brief case with the half of a script he had just written.

At seven, heavily laden with assorted groceries, he arrived at Dotty's apartment.

He waited only to put down the packages. Then he said,

"Dotty, do you think you could write a week of *Millie* scripts for me? Five of them?"

Her eyes opened wide and her lips parted a little. She said, "Why—I—I *think* I could, Bill. I'd love to try it. But why? I mean—"

He said, "It's a big favor to me, if you can do it. I'm tied up in granny knots. I need a week's vacation ten times as bad as I need a week's salary. The salary is all yours for the week. Want to try it?"

"*Do* I? Why, Bill, it's marvelous. I'd *love* to. Are you sure you really—?"

"Positive. It'll keep me out of the loony bin. And I can read over what you do before we turn it in; that much work won't hurt me. And your feelings won't be hurt if I don't like some parts of it, and make you do them over?"

"Why, of course not, Bill. I'll appreciate criticism—and need it. I wouldn't think of turning in scripts without your telling me they were all right. You know so much more about it than I do."

"All right, then. It's a deal. Hungry? I mean, shall we eat right away and talk about it more later, or shall I turn over the scripts to you now?"

"I'm so excited, Bill, I don't care if I ever eat."

"All right." Tracy opened the brief case and pulled out the scripts. He put them on the desk in two piles, a big one and a little one. "These are old scripts, in order, in case you want to refer back to anything. They go back three weeks—if you have to look up any dope further back than that, you'll have to use the files at the studio. And these"—he pointed to the smaller stack—"are the five scripts for this coming week, Monday through Friday. Not played yet. You've read them all, I think, while we were working on the patching up. What you're writing is the week following that, and here's half a script to start on—and the synopsis for the sequence. Wilkins has approved the synopsis, at least enough of it to cover the first week's scripts."

Dotty, her eyes still glowing with excitement, took the uncompleted script and the synopsis.

Tracy said, "Okay, read those if you want, so you can get started thinking about it. I'll start dinner."

"You really wouldn't mind? I *would* like to read these now. And—oh, one thing I should ask. Is the studio to know about this, or don't you want them to?"

"Why not? Sure, I'll tell Wilkins. And I'll arrange to get you a week's leave from your stenographic job if—if I have to cover it myself. No reason why he should object, if the scripts are okay. And I'll go over them and be sure they are."

"But if he *doesn't* agree?"

"We'll do it anyway, except that you'll have to do it evenings instead of getting the week off work. That is, if you can. But don't worry; he won't object. Now I'll rustle us some grub."

Whistling, feeling that tons of weight were off his shoulders, he went to the kitchenette and started opening the packages he had brought.

He kept on whistling while he worked. He felt happier than he had felt in weeks. He heard Dotty go over to the desk and heard keys start to click.

He stuck his head out of the kitchenette. "Starting already?"

"Just retyping the part of a script you wrote, Bill, to get the feel of it. Say, that's a wonderful idea of yours for the quarrel between Millie and Dale. I mean, Millie thinking Dale is making passes at a girl at the office. The redheaded comptometer operator."

"Yeah," said Tracy.

"Is he really making passes, do you think, or does Millie just think so?"

"Well—" said Tracy.

"And how did Millie find out?"

"I've been wondering that myself. Listen, young lady, maybe you can write radio continuity and talk at the same time, but I've got to concentrate in order to get us a dinner here. How long do you have to boil water before you pour it through a dripolator? All right, don't tell me. Let me guess."

Outside the kitchenette there was silence except for the clicking of keys.

CHAPTER 11

TRACY KEPT on whistling, not too far off key, while he worked. This was wonderful, he thought. Out there a typewriter was clicking out *Millie* continuity—retyping it, anyway—and he didn't have to think about it at all. A week of absolute, heaven-sent freedom from soap operas.

A little while later, with a pair of cube steaks beginning to sizzle appetizingly on the stove, he peered around the corner of the kitchenette again. He had a side view of Dotty at the desk, and he leaned against the doorjamb to watch.

Dotty, working hard, was a pretty picture. Somehow she managed to give the impression of a little girl doing her lessons. But, even if she did thrust out her lower lip like a child, the typewriter was taking real punishment. He wished he could type that fast.

Yes, she was cute all right. Cute as a little red wagon. Maybe—

But no, dammit, not this evening. If he made a pass at her now, it would look like a crude demand for repayment for the favor he was doing her by giving her a real chance at radio writing. He'd have to wait a while now. Dammit, why hadn't he made the pass first and then the business proposition?

A smell of something burning made him pull his head back into the kitchenette. He shoved the skillet off the fire with one hand, with the other he grabbed a fork and speared the steaks to lift them from the too-hot skillet. But the bottom sides of the steaks were black and charred, and salvage was hopeless.

Well, luckily he'd bought four of them. He put the burned ones in the step-on can and the remaining steaks into the skillet. And this time he watched the steaks instead of Dotty.

He had the table folded down from the door, set, and ready before he called her. She looked up, startled, as though surprised to see he was still there.

Then she smiled contritely. "Oh, Bill, I should have helped you. I meant to work just a little while and then—"

"I liked doing it," Tracy said. "Anyway, it's ready. Come and get it."

"Mmmm," said Dotty, when she had taken her first bite. "It's good."

"I'll make a fine wife for somebody," Tracy admitted modestly. "How goes the script?"

"I was just starting the second one. I'd like you to read over the first one when we finish eating, Bill. You can do that while I wash the dishes."

Tracy's face went black. "The *second* one? You mean in that little while you typed the half I had done, *wrote* the second half of it, and started another script? While I was rustling grub?"

He looked up at the clock in consternation. It was just eight o'clock; she'd been working less than an hour.

"Uh-huh. And I made a few little changes in retyping the part you wrote; I particularly want to know what you think of them. Just a plant or two to lead to things that will come into the next scripts. And listen, Bill, when we get to the actual accident, don't you think it would be a good idea to have it a hit-run case? And then you've got another complication we can use later. The search for the guilty driver. Whether or not Dale dies, we can use it to lead into another sequence if we wish."

"Sure, why not? Nothing to lose if we don't follow up on it. But dammit, Dotty, in less than an hour, you wrote—say, do you mind if I read that script while I eat?"

She didn't mind.

Tracy read it while he ate. The first part was familiar—too familiar for comfort after the three and three-quarter hour tussle he'd had with it. The changes were minor, as Dotty had said. He spotted a plant or two—a mention of a new girl in Dale's office. A touch of peevishness on Millie's part.

What few changes had been made in the wording were minor

improvements. But all of that was easy; almost anybody can improve a script. One can hardly retype one without seeing a phrase or a sentence here and there that can easily be strengthened.

It was when he got to the new part, the part that was all Dotty's, that he began to read carefully and with such absorption that he forgot to eat. He read it through, slowly.

It was lousy. It smelled. It—

But, wait a minute—*did* it? Leafing back to the middle— partly to reread it, partly to postpone discussing it while he thought—he sat there staring at it. He tried to analyze what was wrong with it, *why* it smelled.

The *writing* was good. The language was good. Conversation was natural. The plot was what he'd already approved.

Then why in hell—?

It wasn't until he was almost finished with the second reading that the answer came to him.

It wasn't Dotty's script that he didn't like—it was simply that it was soap opera, and that soap opera itself was such a ghastly travesty of life. Even *Millie's Millions*. Maybe especially *Millie's Millions*.

Good Lord, while he himself was writing it, he'd been too close to it to see it for what it really was. He'd known that soap opera in general was an insult to the adult intelligence, but he'd kidded himself into thinking that *Millie's Millions* was different and better.

Dammit, he'd been hypnotizing himself; he realized that now. He'd known that he'd been writing trash, but he'd kidded himself out of thinking about it. This half a script of Dotty's was as good—every bit as good—as the ones he'd written. But he'd made the mistake of looking at it objectively because it wasn't his own.

He cut back a couple of pages and read again, this time trying to ignore his own point of view and read it from the point of view of his moronic listeners.

He breathed freely again. Yes, it was good. At any rate, it was up to standard, and that was quite something for anybody's first try. He reached for the opening of the second script and read that. Yes, it was all right, too.

He looked up—daring to do so for the first time—and saw that Dotty was looking at him expectantly and a bit anxiously.

"This is swell, Dotty," he told her. "You do it every bit as well as I do—and a hell of a lot faster."

"Thanks, Bill. You're exaggerating, but—Gee, the way you looked when you read that the first time, I was afraid I'd done it all wrong."

Tracy grinned at her. "That glower was jealousy. Had to read it again to find a few minor flaws to restore my ego. Well, you're off to a flying start with a swell evening's work. And it's early yet; even after we clean the dishes it'll still be early. Shall we see a show? Night club? Take a look at Harlem? Or what?"

"Oh, not tonight, Bill. I'm much too excited about this chance you've given me. I want to stay right at it. I want to finish that second script."

Tracy looked at her incredulously. "You aren't kidding? You mean you really *want* to work? A girl can look like you do and actually enjoy working?"

"That isn't work, Bill! Why, it's fun. Really fun, to write a play that you know thousands and thousands of people are going to hear on the radio and enjoy and—"

"Whoa," said Tracy. "Let's get this straight. You mean that you really *like* writing this sort of thing? And listening to it?"

"Why, of *course*. I listened to *Millie's Millions* almost every day, before I started working at the studio. I never dreamed, then, that someday I'd actually write some scripts for it, Bill. Why, I think that the radio—"

And for the next half hour, Tracy heard quite a bit of what Dotty thought about radio, for she could talk almost as fast as she could write. He heard it and shook his head in blank amazement.

At the end of that time—for Dotty could work and talk simultaneously, and she wouldn't let him help, or even wipe—the dishes were done and the room in order again.

And Tracy found himself being pushed—verbally, if not

physically—out of the door so Dotty could go back to work on the second script.

He reached the sidewalk in somewhat of a daze. He walked home because he wanted to think. He felt slightly drunk with the sheer joy of freedom—of being able to go to bed tonight without *Millie's Millions* hanging over his head. Freedom for a whole blessed week.

Real freedom, for he felt sure now that he wouldn't really have to read the scripts Dotty would write for him, or think a single thought about them. Oh, he'd look them over so he'd have excuses to see Dotty again a few times. He'd even read them, but he wouldn't have to think or worry about them.

And later in the week, when she'd written the full quota of scripts and the business deal was over with—

He got home before nine o'clock.

It was a ghastly hour for Tracy to get home, but he was dead tired, he found. Maybe it was the aftermath of the horrible afternoon he'd spent trying to write. Maybe it was the reaction to the sudden freedom.

He didn't even try to read a while. He almost fell into bed and he was asleep almost before he landed there. He slept dreamlessly; no mares of night perched upon the footboard of his bed to gibber at him that his real troubles hadn't started yet.

*   *   *

Maybe by now it has occurred to you that Tracy would not have made a good detective. He was a nice guy, but he just wasn't the type. He was too easy going. He hadn't the least inclination, ordinarily, to go hunting for trouble. There were so many better things in life for a man to hunt—and not only what you're thinking about. He liked good books and good music and playing cards and chess and seeing plays, if they were good ones, and drinking good liquor in good company. He liked to talk and—when he was with someone who knew something he didn't know and was willing to talk about it—he was even a good listener.

He didn't like people to enact, in bloody reality, murder

131

plans that had been figments of his imagination. They hadn't been very good scripts anyway, he saw now. The more he thought about them, the less he liked them. Would Arthur Dineen and Frank Hrdlicka have been alive today, he wondered, if he had never thought to write scripts about a murderer wearing a Santa Claus suit and about a murderer stuffing a janitor into a cold furnace?

It was a crazy thought, but then the whole setup was crazy. He lay in bed Sunday morning thinking about it and getting himself into a mild case of the willies.

To make things worse, it was seven o'clock of a Sunday morning—an utterly ungodly hour. But he'd gone to sleep at nine the evening before, and he couldn't get back to sleep after ten hours of it.

Resolutely, he pushed murder out of his mind. There wasn't a damn thing he could think of to do about it anyway. And today was his first day in a long time in which he'd have utter freedom from the thought of having to write radio continuity. He meant to enjoy it to the fullest.

And the fullest measure of enjoyment, he thought, would be in doing absolutely nothing at all. At least in planning nothing at all.

He dressed and showered in more leisurely fashion than was his wont and then went downstairs for coffee and the Sunday papers. The latter to read while he drank the former.

Discovery of the theft of the Santa suit from Seabright's had put the Santa Claus murders, as the press now called them, back on the front page. Police promised new developments soon; the nature of the developments was not specified. Tracy read the story in one of the papers, frowning, and then the one in the second paper he'd bought.

The last sentence of the second paper's story made Tracy quit frowning and chuckle instead. "Police are holding an unnamed radio actor as a material witness."

Served Jerry Evers right!

With a lighter heart, he turned to the theatrical section.

132

Three cups of coffee later—it was nine-thirty by more conventional reckoning—he went back to the Smith Arms.

The door of his apartment was slightly ajar. He'd closed and locked it when he left. A little chill of fear went down Tracy's back, and then he pushed the door farther open, and looked in.

Inspector Bates was sitting in the Morris chair, his hat on the desk, and his legs comfortably sprawled out in front of him as he leaned back.

Tracy said, "I really should have knocked, but the door was open. May I come in?"

Bates smiled. "Thought you wouldn't mind if I waited inside instead of out. I still have a passkey."

Tracy went on in and shut the door. He said, "Most Sunday mornings at this time I'm just getting my second wind on sleeping. Anything new?"

"Nothing very startling. I figured you'd be up early; you turned in so early last night."

"Did I?"

"Your light went out at nine twenty-eight. Thought you might like to know we released your friend Jerry Evers this morning. He's in the clear—on the Dineen business anyway. And by my figuring that clears him on the others."

"Others?"

"The other, I mean. Is Evers a publicity hound?"

"Well—he likes ink."

Bates nodded. "I thought so. Then he was probably holding back deliberately on that alibi. He was at his hairdresser's place"—a faint curl of the Inspector's lip commented eloquently—"at the time Dineen was shot. He told us he couldn't remember where he'd been."

"And then changed his mind when you actually held him?"

"No. It came out through routine. We were checking on all his contacts and the hairdresser was on the list. He looked back in his records to see when he'd seen Evers last—and that's how we got it. It seems to be on the up-and-up, too. I was just wondering whether Evers had really forgotten—or if he was just holding back the alibi for an ace in the hole and hoping we'd charge him. Which do you think?"

Tracy said, "I object to the question on the ground that it calls for a statement of opinion on the part of the witness."

Bates stood up and took his hat from the desk. "That's a good enough answer. You should have told us sooner though. That is, if you really want us to find out who did those killings. Well, I'll be seeing you."

He went to the door and put his hand on the knob, then looked around. "By the way, you left your brief case last night."

Tracy didn't think of a good answer until after the door had been closed from the outside. Even then, it wasn't too good an answer.

He sat down and tried to finish reading the papers, but it was tough going. His mind kept asking questions.

Why was Bates having him tailed? Well, he could figure *that* out without a blueprint. But why had Bates gone out of his way to let him know that he was being tailed? That was tougher. In fact, he couldn't even guess a halfway sensible reason.

And if he was being tailed, then Bates must have known he was in Thompson's just now. Why had Bates come up here to wait for him? The conversation had been such that it could have crossed a restaurant table, and the place had been nearly empty, anyway.

He glanced at his desk and saw that the bottom drawer was a little open. He was pretty sure he'd left it closed. He went over to the desk and rummaged through the bottom drawer. The manuscripts were definitely not in the same order in which he'd left them.

All right, that answered that. Bates had come here to check up on Tracy's writing, to make sure he hadn't been dabbling in any more *Murder Can Be Fun* scripts or such.

But why had Bates been careless about how he put the stuff back and closed the drawer? Bates didn't look or act careless. If he hadn't wanted Tracy to know that the desk had been searched, he'd have been careful about it. All right, then, Bates must have wanted him to know.

That settled—or was it?—he managed to finish the parts of the paper he wanted to read.

It was eleven-thirty by then. Time, he thought, that respectable people like Wilkins would certainly be up and about. He might as well get that chore over with, if he could get Wilkins by phone at his home.

He got Wilkins, and Wilkins proved surprisingly agreeable about the week's vacation. Even about letting Dotty have the week off from her regular duties.

"You *are* sure, though, that she can handle it, Mr. Tracy?"

"Absolutely."

"Well—she can't go wrong on the plot if she follows that synopsis you turned in. And if you'll read over the scripts and —ah—polish them up if they need it, it'll be quite all right."

"I'll check up on the scripts before she turns them in. Be glad to do that much. And I'll be around if something comes up—I'm not planning to leave town. I'll probably even drop in at the office once or twice during the week."

"Ah—by the way, Mr. Tracy. I see by the morning papers that a radio actor is being held in connection with that—ah—matter with which you seem to have become—ah—entangled. The name is not mentioned. Do you happen to know if it is someone from our studio?"

"It was, Mr. Wilkins, but it was a false alarm. The police found they were wrong and released him this morning."

"Good. It was Pete Meyer, of course?"

"What? No, it was Jerry Evers. But it was purely a mistake and he has been released."

After he had hung up the receiver, Tracy looked thoughtfully at it for a while. Why had Wilkins assumed that Pete Meyer had been the radio actor who'd been arrested?

He picked up the phone again and called Dotty. She was delighted to learn that Tracy's plan was agreeable to Wilkins.

"So you won't have to report in to work tomorrow," he told her. "You're off for the week—outside of having Millie Mereton on your hands."

"Wonderful, Bill. I've been getting behind in my writing for the magazines. I've had two stories on my mind that I've been wanting to write."

"You can do that and the *Millie* stuff, too? You're sure?"

"Oh, the *Millie* stuff will be easy, Bill. I've got four of them done already. I can finish the other one today—I've got an appointment for this afternoon and this evening but it isn't until two o'clock and that gives me a couple of hours."

"*Four* of them? *Since last night?*"

"Yes, Bill. I wrote two after you left last night and one this morning. Of course you've read only one and the start of the second and you may suggest some improvements. Look, shall I take them in to the office tomorrow morning and meet you there? You can look over all five scripts then and if there's any rewriting I can do it right there and—"

"No!" yelled Tracy. "No! Listen, Dotty—uh—don't you see the spot you're putting me on? If you let the office know Monday that you've got them all done, there won't be any excuse for your being off all week, for one thing, and—for heaven's sake, *no!*"

He thought fast and furiously for a moment. "And there's another angle, Dotty. Wilkins is funny one way—if you bat out something fast, he'll tear it to pieces because you did it that way, whether it's good or not. He has the idea that anything good takes a long time to do."

"Oh. Thanks for telling me that. Well—look, just to let him know I'm really working on it, I'll drop in tomorrow and turn in the one script you've read, the first one. I'll let him think I spent the week end writing it—and then rewriting it after you'd read the first draft. Will that be all right?"

"Sure, fine. And I'll phone you tomorrow and we can arrange to get together so I can read the other scripts."

"All right, Bill. 'Bye."

This time he didn't sit staring at the phone; he went into the kitchen and poured himself a drink.

He was sweating a little. What the hell right did a dimwit like Dotty—and she *was* a dimwit or she couldn't *like* soap operas—have to possess the ability to turn out continuity like a sausage machine turns out sausage—a foot a second—while a smart guy like him had to *sweat* the stuff out?

Damn the wench.

Well, Millie Wheeler would be up by now. He wasn't going to cry on her shoulder; not for a million bucks would he go to her for solace in this particular sorrow. But if he stayed alone any longer, he'd start peeling paper off the walls.

Millie was home, and up. She saw his face and said, "Tracy, what's wrong?"

"Wrong? Nothing at all."

"Sit down and tell mama. And while you tell, there's some bourbon in the cupboard and ginger ale in the icebox. Or would you rather have it straight?"

"Either way. Nothing's wrong, Millie. Fact is, I was just going to suggest we go out and celebrate. I'm free for a week."

"And then what? You go to jail?"

"Such language. I mean free from *Millie's Millions*. I've been on the verge of the screaming meamies, and—uh— through Wilkins I found somebody who'd take over the continuity writing for a week."

"Oh. Tracy, that *is* good news. But can you—uh—?"

"Afford it? Sure. There's a few hundred in the bank. Not a fortune, but I won't starve."

Millie had been mixing the drinks. She brought them. "That wasn't what I meant. Are the police going to be stuffy about your leaving town? I hear they sometimes are, when there's a murder case. And you ought to get away somewhere. Province-town's nice in August. Why don't you go up there?"

Tracy took a meditative sip at his highball. He said, "Funny, but I never thought of getting away. Now that I do think about it, I don't really want to. Know why?"

"No. Why?"

He sipped the highball again. "The essence of freedom is to be able to remain in the environment in which one ordinarily has to work—*without* having to work. I'm going to leave the cover off my typewriter all week, so I can thumb my nose at it every time I go by."

"Ummm," said Millie. "You might have something there. But also, the essence of freedom is *not* to sit around with your face a yard long. Are we going out to celebrate or to drown a secret sorrow you won't tell me about? Which?"

Tracy sighed, and then managed to grin. He said, "All right, toots; we'll celebrate. But let's get back to this vacation idea of mine, spent in the same environment. I think I've got something there."

"What?"

"Take an office worker, for instance, who has to sit at a desk eight hours a day. What would best bring home to him his sense of freedom during a vacation? Going out of town? No. Sticking around and going down to the office every day—or almost every day. Not for eight hours, of course. He'd set his alarm clock for the usual time so he could have the pleasure of shutting it off and going back to sleep.

"When he did get up, he'd go down to the office, late as hell and not having to care about it. Think of the freedom of being able to walk in at ten-thirty or eleven and sit down at his desk, without it mattering at all!"

"Go on," said Millie.

"And he sits down at his desk and puts his feet up on it—not having to worry for fear the boss is watching him, or for fear his work won't get done—because he hasn't any work to do. Why, the psychic satisfaction of just *sitting* there, doing nothing, knowing he can get up and walk out any time he decides to—it'd do him a thousand times more good and make him feel a thousand times better than going out of town and coming back a physical wreck."

"With sunburn and poison ivy."

"And chigger bites and his money gone because he drank too much in that upstate roadhouse and tried to beat the one-armed bandit."

"Tracy, it *is* an idea. I'll bet you could sell an article about it if you wrote one, in the right vein. Not too serious and not too farcical. Keep the reader guessing whether you're kidding or on the level. I'll bet you could sell it to one of the top mags."

Tracy laughed. "Now you're getting commercial. Come on, let's get going."

While Millie got ready, he went across the hall for his hat. He was feeling swell now. Solemnly he took the cover off the Underwood and thumbed his nose at it.

Then he winced at the unbidden thought of another typewriter which—at this very moment—was undoubtedly clicking out the final script of *Millie* continuity for next week at the rate of a page every seven minutes, like clockwork.

He put the thought away from him and went back to get Millie Wheeler.

They had a few drinks, and then ate. They had a few drinks and then stopped in at the Martin to dance. But the music turned out to be too good to dance to. They sat and listened, and talked, and had a few more drinks.

And when—at six—Millie had to leave because of a previous appointment, they were reasonably sober and it had been a magic afternoon. Anyway, it had been fun. Neither murder nor radio had been mentioned once.

Not until he left Millie at her apartment. She kissed him lightly and then, a hand still on his arm, looked at him very seriously.

"Tracy," she said, "you'll be careful, won't you?"

"Careful?"

"You know what I mean. You didn't want to talk about it, I could see, so I didn't. But you can't fool mama. You got out from under your radio writing for a week so you could find out who killed Dineen and Frank."

Tracy was startled. "Did I?"

"Of course you did. And I don't blame you. It does seem that the police aren't getting anywhere at all. But do be careful, Tracy. Listen—"

"I'm listening."

"I've got a hunch, Tracy. The police think whoever killed them is a psychopathic killer, a homicidal maniac."

Tracy said, "With me, that's an odds-on favorite."

"But *he isn't*. Tracy, there's a motive back of those killings.

139

Maybe I'm fey, or maybe I'm a little goofy, but I can feel it. There's a cold, calculating killer back of them, I'm sure. I haven't the faintest idea why, what the motive is, but I'm sure. And if you start to find it, he'll kill *you*, Tracy, if he can."

Tracy gulped. He said, "Well—I'll not let him know I'm working on it."

"But you will, in spite of yourself. You'll be asking people questions; that's the only way you can find out things and try to fit them together. *You'll be asking the murderer questions, too.* Because you don't know who he is, but he must be someone you know."

"But—"

"It's got to be, Tracy. Someone who knows you well. Everything points to that. Someone who knows you as well as I do."

Tracy's guard was down. He said, "Not quite that well, Millie," and reached to put his arm around her again. But her hands against his chest held him off.

She said, "Don't you see how dangerous it will be to meddle with it, Tracy? For all you know, it might be me. Don't you remember, I'm the only one besides yourself you know read that Santa Claus script before the first murder?"

"Don't be silly."

"I'm not being silly, Tracy. No, I didn't do it. But I'm afraid —for you. You say you'll be careful, but how can you be careful unless you have at least an idea who to be careful of?"

"But—"

"I'm not trying to stop you. I know how you must feel about it. You've got to try—and I wouldn't like you if you didn't feel that way. But if there's any way I can help, let me. Will you?"

"Sure," Tracy said. "Sure, Millie."

Then the pressure of her hands against his chest relaxed and he kissed her again. She slipped inside, and closed the door.

Tracy stood there trying to decide whether he was going into his own apartment or outside again. It should have been an easy decision, one way or the other, but he was too confused at the moment to make it. He was a little bewildered at Millie's interpretation of his motives and character, and he was more than a little frightened.

Or could Millie have been right? *Had* trying to solve this mess been at the back of his mind in his decision to arrange for a week free from work?

Hell, no. It hadn't. What could he, Tracy, hope to do that the police—with all their facilities and all their experience—couldn't do? Especially now that Jerry Evers' little stunt had blown up in Jerry's face and the police weren't any longer wasting time on Jerry. That was the only edge he'd ever had on them; the only thing he'd ever known that they hadn't.

Dammit, that's what the police were *for*, solving crimes. He, Tracy, wasn't a detective and didn't claim to be. Damn Millie for putting him on a spot like that!

And why, Tracy asked Tracy, didn't you let Millie know she was wrong about why you took the week off? And Tracy couldn't tell Tracy the answer to that, because Tracy knew it already.

Anyway, he needed a drink and didn't want to have it alone in his apartment.

He went downstairs and outside again. It was dusk; there was a pleasant cool breeze. It was a nice evening, or could have been.

He stood there, wondering which way to go, just as he'd stood there a few evenings ago when Mrs. Murdock had introduced herself to him and he'd been shown the scene of the crime in the basement.

And darned if—yes, that was she coming now around the corner. Dressed just as she had been dressed Thursday evening. But she didn't come rushing and gushing this time. She saw him, stopped abruptly, and then scurried into the door of Thompson's like a gopher popping into a hole.

It should have been funny, Tracy told himself.

It wasn't.

Scaring her that way had been a damn silly idea. He had a hunch Bates' serious suspicion of him had dated from that moment. And it wasn't fun being thought a psychopathic killer, either by a Mrs. Murdock or by the police. Particularly by the police.

He swore softly to himself and started walking. He went by Thompson's without looking in, so that Mrs. Murdock—who would be looking out—would see him pass and know the coast was clear for her to scurry home to her insurance-agent husband and her radio serials. He owed her that much anyway, no matter how dowdy and silly she was.

Could Frank have been having an affair with her? He hoped not, for Frank's sake. Not that it mattered to Frank now. Nothing mattered after you were dead.

And all that mattered, really, while you were alive was keeping that way and keeping out of trouble, and trying to enjoy each day as it came, and not missing anything out of life that you didn't have to miss, and—oh, hell.

Damn all women.

Damn Mrs. Murdock for having been so silly as to have led *him* to act even sillier.

Damn Dotty for being able—why not be honest about it?— to write just as good radio continuity with, as it were, one hand, as he could write with two hands and the use of a cudgel on his brains. And double damn her for being so pretty and sweet and desirable that she didn't *look* as though she knew how to spell words over one syllable. Damn her for being so brilliant—and, yet so incredibly stupid that she could *like* to write stuff that should make any intelligent person shudder.

Damn Millie Mereton on all counts, and damn Millie Wheeler for trying to make a hero out of him when he was just a heel.

He was in a lousy mood, and he knew it. He walked past Dick Kreburn's hotel without even looking up to see if Dick's window was lighted, because he knew at the moment he wasn't fit company for man or beast, let alone a nice guy like Dick.

He kept on walking, and there was the *Blade* Building, and he could hear the dim rumble of the presses. He glowered and kept on going. He passed Barney's place—then hesitated, went

142

back and went in. After all, he had to light somewhere, sometime.

Barney's was empty, except for Barney. Sitting down at the bar, Tracy didn't know whether he was glad about that or not. He was in a mood to tell somebody off—and anybody from the *Blade* who wanted to wisecrack about his present occupation would be a perfect victim.

He said, "Barney, two double bourbons, and no humor. Water for a wash."

Barney brought the bottle, shaking his head lugubriously. "That ain't the way to drink, Tracy. Not for a guy like you."

"What about a guy like me?"

"You're a gentleman."

"Oh," said Tracy. He sniffed around it suspiciously. It could have been an insult, but Barney hadn't meant it that way.

He said, "You're dead wrong, Barney. I'm a heel.

"You're drunk, Tracy."

"You're wrong again. I've been drinking like a gentleman all afternoon. Gentlemen don't get stinking drunk, and I intend to get stinking drunk. Have one with me, Barney. Have two with me."

"Well—a short one."

"Mud in your eye."

Tracy put down the first glass and closed his hand over the second one. He took a deep breath and downed that one too.

He felt that second one. The afternoon of drinking like a gentleman had laid a nice foundation.

For a moment he seemed to be looking at himself from a long way off, as though he saw himself through the wrong end of a telescope. The sight saddened him.

He said again, "Barney, I'm no gentleman. I'm a heel."

Barney grinned. "A heel doesn't know he's a heel. If a guy knows he's a heel, then he ain't."

It sounded sensible, and then it didn't. He tried to analyze it and it seemed to go around in a circle.

Barney was leaning forward across the bar. He said, "What's

wrong with you, Tracy? Anything I can do? Aren't short of money, are you?"

"Money? Hell no, Barney. I've even got the stuff in the bank. It's not like the old days."

"It ain't at that." Barney chuckled. "You used to owe me five or ten out of every check you got. Well, if you're in the bucks, it ain't money. Is it women?"

"I've heard the word somewhere. What does it mean?"

Barney scratched his head. "Used to have some French post-cards around with women on 'em. If I knew where, I could show you. Say, Tracy, I just remembered. Randolph."

"Lee? What about him?"

"I mentioned you were in here the other day. Said if you dropped around again, he wanted to see you about something. Okay if I call him up and tell him you're here?"

"I guess so. If you promised him you would."

"Want to go up to his office if he wants you to, or want him to come here? That is, if he's still in the office—he said some-thing about working tonight."

Tracy shrugged. "Either way. Leave it up to him."

Barney went back to the phone.

CHAPTER 12

TRACY POURED himself another shot—a single one this time. The two doubles had given him an edge, pushed him just a little over the border. Now he'd better slow down or he'd end up like he had at Stan's place Thursday night.

Thursday night—Hell, Thursday night he'd seen Mrs. Mur-dock, just as he had tonight. He'd passed Dick's place; he'd been to the *Blade;* he'd been to Barney's; he'd ended up drunk.

Was tonight going to repeat the identical itinerary? Should he head for Stan's place tonight too, just for the hell of it? Was there a Fate that—Cut it out, he told himself; you're getting drunk when you start thinking about Fate with a capital letter.

He poured another drink. He was feeling a little better now. Some of the bitterness was going out of him. He was glad now that he'd stopped in Barney's.

Barney came back. He said, "Lee's going to drop in here. He's on his way down." He picked up the bottle and put it on the back bar. "You're hitting them a little fast, Tracy."

Tracy sighed. "All right, Grandma. Anyway, I can still count." He put a bill on the bar. "Two doubles, two singles, and your own."

Barney rang it up and came back with the change. Tracy picked up a nickel of it and went over to the juke box. He looked over the listings and then turned around. He said, "My God, Barney, the *Beer Barrel Polka's* still on her. The one we used to play half a dozen times a night. Don't tell me it's the same record and not worn through to the other side?"

"New record, but the same version. You boys wore that one out all right. Jeez, how I used to hate the thing."

"Me too," said Tracy. He dropped his nickel and pushed the button for the *Beer Barrel Polka*. He came back to the bar and sat down as it started.

The same damn tune. But it made him wish the gang was in here right now, and that they were playing pinochle and drinking beer at the back table. Hell, they *would* be in tonight around eleven, and it was now—He looked at the clock. Only seven-fifteen.

The city editor of the *Blade* came in just as the record finished. "That damn tune," he said. "Tracy, your taste hasn't improved a bit."

"*My* taste!" said Tracy indignantly. "I always did hate that thing. What you drinking?"

"Just a beer. Got to go back to work."

"And another shot for me, Barney, if I've been a good boy long enough. What's cooking, Lee?"

"Well—first, let's get this over with, one way or the other.

That story Bates gave us, about the scripts of yours being followed out in the murders. Was it straight stuff?"

"Absolutely, Lee. And except for minor details, it's the whole damn truth, as far as I know."

"Is it? That's what I wanted to see you about. There's at least one more story in it, if we can get enough dope to fill it out. The Mueller angle. Walther Mueller."

Suddenly Tracy wished he was a little more sober. He shook his head to clear it, and it didn't help much. He asked, "How'd you find out about that?"

"Through you. Tracy, did you ever write a script about a jeweler getting murdered?"

Tracy nodded slowly. He said, "All right, I'll talk first. Then you tell me how you got onto it, and what you know." He told Randolph about Bates asking if he'd ever heard of a Walther Mueller—and Bates asking whether he'd been in town the first week in June. He said, "I put the two together and looked over the newspapers for that week and found the news account of the murder. That's all I know. And it's a false alarm, Lee. Just because I wrote a script about a jeweler, Bates was checking back on the last jeweler to be killed in town. That's all. The method was different, and everything."

"Sure of that?"

"Positive. How'd you find out about it?"

"Through you, like I said. Ray, down in Circulation, told me he'd given you back copies for that week. I looked through them myself to see what had interested you. There were several murders in the news that week. I checked into all of 'em and the Mueller one was the only one that tied in."

"But it didn't, I tell you. It was just—"

"Barney," said Lee, "Another beer. And a shot for my inebriated ex-employee. He's going to need it."

He tapped a finger against the top button of Tracy's vest. He said, "If you'd been a reporter instead of a—what you are—you'd have checked who handled the funeral arrangements. I did. It was an old-established undertaking outfit by the name of Westphal & Boyd."

Tracy said, "I'm suitably amazed. So what?"

"So next I did what you'd have done if you'd been on the ball. I checked with Wesphal & Boyd to see who handed them the funeral arrangements to handle, and I found out."

"I'll bet a little Boyd told you."

Randolph winced. "I should walk out on you. Better, I should poke you in the nose. But instead, I'll tell you. The man who made the arrangements with the mortuary was named Dineen. Arthur D. Dineen."

Tracy took a long deep breath. He let it out slowly. He felt sober suddenly. He said. "And what else? You didn't stop there."

Lee said, "I went to Bates with what I had, and he wouldn't tie any ribbons on it for me. He wouldn't cooperate even enough to tell me why he wouldn't cooperate."

"When was this, Lee?"

"Yesterday. So I sent Burke out to talk to Mrs. Dineen to see what he could get there. It was something, but not much. She's the kind of a dame who hates reporters and froze up. Burke made the guess that she didn't want the past raked over, because she was afraid something might come out. Like maybe Dineen was playing around with someone. Was he?"

"I don't know, Lee. I heard a rumor but I don't know."

"But we found out this much: Dineen and this Walther Mueller were close friends. Before Dineen got into radio, when he was younger, he'd lived in South America. He'd represented an American firm there. He and Mueller had formed a friendship that stuck, even after Dineen came back. He'd been back to South America a time or two on vacations, and Mueller had been here a time or two. And they'd corresponded."

"Did Dineen meet Mueller at the plane?"

Randolph shook his head. "His wife says not. Says they'd known Mueller was coming to America, this time to stay, but they didn't know exactly when he was to arrive. Mueller went right from the plane to the hotel and was killed there before he'd even phoned Dineen—and they didn't know Mueller was in town yet until they read about the murder in the papers. At least that's what Mrs. Dineen says. Anyway, Dineen stepped in then, helped in winding up Mueller's affairs, arranging the funeral and what not."

"Ummm," said Tracy. "Did Mueller have, any relatives?"

"A son and two daughters back in Rio de Janeiro—all grown up and married—inherited the estate. It wasn't too big—somewhere in five figures, but he wasn't a millionaire. Dineen was executor for the estate. Officially, I mean—actually he let his lawyer handle it."

"You saw the lawyer?"

"Burke did, this morning. Nothing startling. The pearl necklace that was in customs at the time of the murder was turned over to the estate and brought twelve thousand, after the duty was paid. Then there was the bank draft he brought with him, and a few investments back in Rio. Came to about thirty thousand after all deductions and all goes back to Rio, to the son and the daughters."

Tracy made slow circles on the bar with the wet bottom of his shot glass. He asked, "Any relatives in this country?"

"A niece. Mrs. Dineen said she believed she lived in Hartford, Connecticut. Mrs. Dineen never met her."

"Know her name?"

"No. What the hell could that matter?"

That might depend, Tracy thought, on what the name was. But he didn't say it. He said, "Couldn't, I guess. That's all you've got?"

"Listen who's asking! Sure it's all I've got. But one thing puzzles me. Why isn't Bates hotter on that angle than he is?"

Tracy stared at his reflection in the back-bar mirror. He said, "I guess because Bates thinks it doesn't really tie in. He thinks he knows who killed Dineen and Hrdlicka."

"The hell. Who?"

"Me," said Tracy. "I think he thinks I'm psychopathic. That I write scripts and then feel impelled to act them out. Or something."

"Are you?"

"Don't be an ass, Lee. Would I tell you, if I was?"

Lee Randolph shook his head wonderingly. He said, "I know you pretty well, I guess. You aren't crazy—that way. But what are you going to do about it?"

"What *can* I do about it? Nothing. Except not let Bates catch me at any more murders."

"You're not kidding me, Tracy? You really mean, you're just sitting on your dead ass hoping you'll be cleared? Dammit, Tracy, you used to be a good reporter."

"What's being a reporter got to do with it?"

Randolph snorted. "When you worked for me, if I'd put you on a case like this, you'd have gone around asking people questions till you got some answers that dovetailed—or didn't. Then you'd—Oh, skip it. I hope Bates sends you up."

"A lot of consolation *you* are."

"Consolation," said Randolph. "That's what you want, huh? For God's sake, consolation. Somebody uses you for a fall guy for three murders or so, and you sit on your fanny and want consolation. If that's what radio does to a good reporter, I'll take mustard."

"Goddam it, Lee, you can't—"

"The hell I can't. You've turned softer than a featherbed. What you need is a deadline. Okay, I'll give you one. Get me the story by tomorrow night, or you're fired."

Tracy grinned. "Simon Legree, my pal. Glad I don't work for you any more."

"I'm damn glad, too," Randolph said. He tossed down the rest of his beer and stood up.

He said, "You used to be a hell of a guy once. Now you want consolation."

He walked out of the tavern.

Tracy's grin faded slowly. He watched it fade in the back-bar mirror, and then motioned to Barney.

"A double," he said. He turned and looked at the windows at the front. It was dark outside now. It wasn't any too bright inside.

He said, "Dammit, Barney—"

"Yeah?"

And what was the answer to that? He didn't know the answer to anything. He said, "Have one with me, Barney."

Barney poured it. He said "Bumps" and they drank.

Tracy said, "Barney, I used to be a good reporter once."

"Yeah," said Barney. There wasn't any question mark after the "Yeah" this time and it annoyed Tracy that there wasn't. It would also have annoyed him if there was.

"So what?" he said.

"So nothing," Barney said. "I was just agreeing with you. Thanks for the drink." He moved off down the bar to wipe some glasses.

I'm going to get drunk, Tracy thought. Hell, I *am* drunk. Or am I?

He didn't know. Physically, there was that woozy feeling that comes with one too many, but there didn't seem to be any cobwebs in his brain. His body was just a little drunk; he knew that when he got off the stool he'd have to concentrate to walk naturally. But his mind was still at the wrong end of that damn telescope, looking through at a tiny Tracy sitting alone at the bar, trying to get drunk.

"Look—" he said.

"Yeah?" Barney looked toward him but didn't come back.

"It's none of their goddam business."

Barney just grunted.

Barney must think he was drunk, talking like that. Maybe Barney was right. He shouldn't use a pronoun without an antecedent.

But it *wasn't* their business.

What right had Millie to assume that he had taken this week's freedom to stick his nose into a buzz saw? It was his nose, not Millie's.

And what business was it of Lee Randolph's to think he ought to go mixing himself up worse in something he was too mixed up in already? He paid city taxes, didn't he, for the upkeep of a police department whose business it was to solve crimes. And they had facilities for solving them, and he didn't.

What right did Barney have to agree with them? Yes, Barney did; he could tell by the way Barney looked at him.

Bates was more sensible. Bates wouldn't think he was taking a week off to hunt a killer. Hell, no. Bates would think he was taking time off to figure out another murder or two.

Damn that telescope he saw himself through. Damn the mirror back of the bar. It showed him another bar and a solitary, owl-eyed drunk sitting at it alone, looking like a dope. Just a dope at twilight, when the lights are low.

A dope who let himself be pushed around by the police, because a killer had pushed him around first. A damned plagiaristic killer who'd stolen his ideas.

A three-time killer, at least. Sure, admit it. The Mueller business was in, too. Mueller had been a friend of Dineen. That was enough of a tie-up to put it into the pattern somewhere.

Coincidence; that was what you called a clue that you were too lazy or too scared to run down.

Like Dotty-Dorothea Mueller. Dotty the beautiful, with the soft neck nape that had been so nice to kiss, and with the flying fingers that could turn a typewriter into a machine gun. Little and soft and tender and young and desirable and—*damn* her.

Her last name being Mueller wasn't any coincidence. There weren't any coincidences. A coincidence was the name you put on a lead you were afraid to follow up.

Randolph would have followed it up all right—or sent one of his leg men to do it—if Randolph had happened to know that a girl named Mueller had worked at KRBY under Dineen, hired by Dineen. Only Randolph hadn't known that; that was one edge he had on Randolph if he decided to get busy and—

But he wasn't going to decide that.

He said, "Another drink, Barney. You too."

Barney came back and poured a drink for him. He said, "Not me this time. The evening's young, it ain't eight o'clock yet. I can't get drunk this early."

"Wherein we differ, Barney. I can. I'm going to."

"Why?"

Tracy said, "Well—" and didn't quite know how to go on. It was a hell of a question for a bartender to ask. It wasn't any of Barney's business *why* a customer wanted to drink.

Why couldn't other people keep from minding his, Tracy's, business, anyway? All he wanted was to be let alone.

He said, "Come back here, Barney."

Barney came back.

Tracy said, "Look, Barney, *is* it anybody's goddam business but mine whether I'm a man or a mouse?"

"I guess it ain't," said Barney. "Which are you?"

"A mouse," Tracy said promptly. "Look, I *like* being a mouse. Look, I'm Bill Tracy, not Dick Tracy. Not Superman. Not even Philo Vance or the guy who took a message to Garcia."

"Who was he?"

"I don't know," said Tracy. "I don't even know who Garcia was or what the message was about. Maybe it was from Garcia's tailor saying he should call for his pants. But this guy took it. I wouldn't have."

Barney said, "I don't know this guy Garcia, but I got a box of Garcia cigars. Want one?"

"Keep it, and don't tempt me to tell you what to do with it."

"You can't smoke a cigar that way," said Barney.

Tracy frowned. He said, "I'm trying to be serious, Barney. How did we get off the track to talking about how you can't smoke a cigar?"

"Garcia. You were not taking a message to Garcia and I told you we had some Garcia cig—"

"Cut it out. Get back to the main question. If I want to be a mouse, and like being a mouse, is it anybody's goddam business but mine?"

"I guess not."

"All right then," said Tracy. "Shut up about it."

Barney sighed and went back to wiping glasses.

Tracy looked at himself in the mirror. It looked, for the moment, as though there were two mice sitting there instead of one, and he had to focus his eyes to resolve the double image.

But why, he thought, go to the trouble? Why couldn't he be two mice if he wanted to? Wasn't there something about two mice being better than one? No, that was heads.

"Barney," he said, "I used to be a good reporter once."

"Yeah," said Barney. There was resignation in his voice.

"Barney."

"Yeah?"

"Barney, are two mice better than one?"

"No."

Tracy said, "That's what I thought."

He got down off the stool and stood there for a moment, resting his hand on the bar in case he'd need it to balance himself. No, he didn't. He could stand up. He could still walk.

If he concentrated, he could even walk straight. He did; he walked straight to the door and out of it.

It was twelve blocks to Dotty's place. He knew he could sober up quite a bit in twelve blocks.

Halfway there, he began to feel almost sober. Almost, too, he decided to turn around and go back.

It was too beautiful a night to start trouble, to go asking for trouble. The breeze was cool and pleasant on his face, as soft as would be the caress of Dotty's hand. And the sky was clear and blue-black, with the stars showing even through the haze of city lights. Stars that were like the little highlights he'd like to see in Dotty's eyes when she looked at him.

Overhead, as he cut across Washington Square, the leaves of the trees rustled, and lovers sat on the benches under them. Children ran and squealed and shrieked.

And it was still a beautiful night when he reached Dotty's.

He went into the hallway, rang the bell and stood with his hand on the knob of the inner door until the latch clicked.

Then he went up the stairs, not having to walk carefully now, and at the top of the stairs he almost changed his mind—not about going on, but about what he was going to do when he got there.

She heard his footsteps along the hall and opened the door.

"Why, Bill! I wasn't expecting—"

He walked on in, past her.

Her voice took on an edge. "Bill, I'm glad to see you, but—I'm sorry, you can't stay. I'm expecting someone else and I was just—"

"I'm not staying," Tracy said.

He glanced over at the desk. The cover was on the typewriter. Beside it lay two neat piles of paper, one pile yellow, the other white. Paper clips divided each pile into five separate manuscripts.

"You finished," he said. His voice sounded accusing, although he hadn't intended that it should.

"Yes, I have. If you want to read them, you may take them along. Your brief case is still here."

Tracy turned and looked at her. She'd closed the door, but she was standing near it. She looked annoyed, and a little puzzled.

He said, "You're from Hartford, aren't you?"

"Yes. What's that go to do with—?"

"Nothing. You had an uncle, then, named Walther Mueller. He was killed a little over two months ago."

"Of course. It was in the papers. Mr. Tracy, what are you trying to say? What's that got to do with—? Have you been drinking?"

"Sure I've been drinking. Look, have you anything to conceal about the matter? Or are you willing to talk about it?"

"Bill, I don't know what you're driving at. Of course I have nothing to conceal about it. How could I have?"

"I don't know. That's what I want to find out."

"What *are* you talking about?"

"Murder," Tracy said. "I'm talking about murders—a lot of murders. Your uncle was murdered. Your boss—the man who hired you at the studio—was murdered. And a friend of mine, a janitor, was mur—Dotty, do you by any chance have any Polish ancestry, way back?"

She took a step backward, clear against the door. Her hand was on the knob. She said, "Bill, you're—tight. I'm sorry, but you'll have to leave. I can't talk to you now. If you want to come tomorrow, when you're not in this mood, I'll be glad to tell you anyth—"

"Have you? Any Polish ancestry?"

"No, of course not. Belgian, on my father's side, and English-Norwegian on my mother's. Now will you go?"

"Did you know a man named Frank Hrdlicka?"

"Frank—That's the man who was killed in the building you live in, wasn't it? The janitor?"

"Yes. Did you ever meet him?"

"Of course not. Mr. Tracy, I *won't* answer questions when you're acting the way you are now."

Tracy said, "If I wasn't feeling this way, Dotty, I wouldn't ask them. But—oh, all right, I apologize. In advance. Now tell me—how did you happen to get that job at KRBY? Through your uncle?"

"Yes. In a way."

"What do you mean, in a way? Did you know Dineen through him?"

"It came about perfectly naturally, Mr. Tracy. But I haven't time—If you'll come tomorrow, I'll tell you about it. Not now."

Tracy said, "It'll take you five minutes to tell it, at the most, if you start in and keep going. You can get me out in five minutes that way. If you want to send for the police, they can be here in fifteen."

She glared at him. Her eyes were like blue marbles now, and there weren't any stars in them.

Tracy sat down on the sofa and pretended to lean back comfortably.

And, abruptly and surprisingly, Dotty smiled at him. She shrugged her shoulders in mock resignation and came closer to sit on the arm of the chair facing the sofa.

She said, "All right, Bill. I'll take into consideration that you've been drinking and not be angry. There's no reason why I shouldn't tell you, except the way you asked, and I'll overlook that. I can tell it in less than five minutes and then—you'll go? Promise?"

"Yes."

"All right. First, I never met my uncle. I knew, though, that I *had* an uncle who had money—I thought it was more than it turned out to be—in South America. About six months ago, when I began to sell love stories, I wrote to him. I suggested—well, that travel would be good experience for a writer and I wondered if—well—"

Tracy said, "Be frank about it. You fished for an invitation to go to Rio and live there for awhile. And he didn't fall for it?"

She frowned a little. "He wrote back that he was leaving there very shortly to come to America to retire. He said he looked forward to meeting me when he got here and—well—he hinted he might be able to do something for me in the way of enabling me to travel. I don't know what he had in mind, and I guess now I never will know.

"But in the same letter he asked me if I was interested in radio writing. He said he had a close friend named Arthur Dineen who was program manager at KRBY, and that if I was interested in radio, why didn't I talk to Mr. Dineen about it and that he'd write Mr. Dineen meanwhile.

"So I came to New York and talked to Mr. Dineen and he gave me the job there. He said I should work in the office a while until I got the feel of things and then he'd try to get me a chance to work on some program.

"So that's all there was to it. I started working there three—no, three and a half months ago."

"Oh," said Tracy. He felt vaguely disappointed, and a little ashamed of himself for having been so abrupt with Dotty. Her story was undoubtedly true. It made sense and it fitted all the facts perfectly.

He asked, "Did either you or Mr. Dineen know when your uncle was coming?"

"I didn't, no. And Mr. Dineen told me afterward that he didn't. He said he wished uncle had wired him so he could have met the plane and that—maybe it would never have happened."

She held out her hand, back up, to show a ring on her fourth finger. "He was bringing me a present—this ring. It's only an

156

aquamarine, but the mounting is beautiful workmanship in white gold."

"It's beautiful," Tracy said. He was feeling a bit foolish now. "The newspapers didn't mention it. How come it wasn't stolen with his money?"

"It was in the customs, of course, like the pearls. There were some other small things that the papers didn't bother to mention—a beautiful silver inkstand for Mr. Dineen, for one thing, and a few other little things."

"How could—how did you know what was intended for whom?"

"He'd declared them that way, for the customs. I mean, they ask whether an object is brought in as a gift or for resale, or for what. The pearls—I guess you read about them—were brought here to sell. He thought he could do better on them here, I guess, even with the duty."

"An inkstand," Tracy said thoughtfully. "That's what the man who killed Dineen took from his office. Was it very valuable?"

"It was silver. The workmanship was exquisite. I don't know; it might have been worth a few hundred, but not more. He—the killer, I mean—would hardly have *gone* there to steal it, but it was certainly valuable enough to take along with him if—"

"Did your uncle bring any other presents for the Dineens or for you?"

"Not for me. I didn't hear about any others. He'd sent Mr. Dineen presents before, though, or given them to him. That wrist watch Mr. Dineen wore, with the sweep second hand. And—did you know Rex? That beautiful dog collar; it was peccary pigskin from South America with gold-plated studs. Mr. Dineen had Rex with him when he visitd South America last spring, and afterward my uncle had the collar made and sent it for Rex. And Mr. Dineen mentioned earrings my uncle had once sent for Mrs. Dineen and—I believe, a clock."

"Wasn't he pretty free with presents?"

"Well, Mr. Dineen had done him some favors. In a business

way, I mean, in New York, and wouldn't take any payment for them. But he couldn't very well turn down presents."

"What sort of favors?"

"I don't know. I haven't an idea." Dotty looked at the clock, very pointedly. "You said five minutes, Bill, and it's been over ten. Honestly, that's *all* I know about it, except what was in the papers."

Tracy stood up. He said, "Sure, thanks. I'll go." He felt considerably like a fool. Obviously Dotty didn't know a thing and her connection with events was perfectly innocent, and he'd started out questioning her as though she were a criminal. It was a wonder she hadn't called the cops to chase him out.

He'd come in like a lion and now he'd go out like a lamb, after having been a mouse—

"What's so funny?" Dotty asked. The edge was coming back to her voice.

"Nothing," said Tracy. "I was just thinking—Say, Dotty, why didn't Dineen tell his wife about your starting to work at the studio?"

It had been a random question, to Tracy.

But Dotty's face suddenly flamed and then went white, and her hand—the one with the aquamarine ring on its fourth finger—flew up and smacked sharply against Tracy's cheek.

"Get out!" she said.

Tracy got out. There just wasn't anything to say. But outside the door, he turned. There still wasn't anything to say but he said, "Well, Dotty, it was nice knowing you. I'm sor—"

The door slammed.

He walked thoughtfully to the stairs. Sure, he was sorry, but he wasn't quite sure what he was sorry about. He'd asked a random question, and it had hit home. Only a guilty conscience could have caused a sudden flare-up like that.

Dineen and Dotty.

Damn.

And he, Tracy, had been chivalrous. He'd acted like a perfect little gentleman. Little Lord Fauntleroy Tracy. Damn.

He went down the stairs and opened the door to the outer hallway.

A dapper little man with graying hair and gold-rimmed, pince-nez glasses was standing there in the hallway, his hand raised to push a door buzzer button. He saw Tracy and hurriedly lowered his hand.

Tracy grinned at him. He bowed slightly from the waist, and then recovered his balance by putting his hand against the wall.

He said, "Good evening, Mr. Wilkins."

"Ah—good evening, Mr. Tracy."

"Good evening, Mr. Wilkins."

"Good—" Wilkins frowned.

"It *is* a good evening," said Tracy. "It's Apartment Seven, in case you're looking. She has the manuscripts ready."

"The—ah—"

"The *Millie* scripts. That's what you came for, of course. And will you tell her I said it was fun just seeing her?"

Wilkins stepped back as Tracy passed him. Wilkins frowned and then pressed the button over mailbox seven. The latch of the inner door clicked just as Tracy opened the outer door.

Tracy leaned back in. He said, "Mr. Wilkins."

"Yes?"

"Watch out for the biological urge. Station KRBY definitely does not approve of its—ah—employees—"

Wilkins had recovered his dignity. His voice was frosty. "That will do, Mr. Tracy."

"Quite, Mr. Wilkins. Good night, Mr. Wilkins."

CHAPTER 13

TRACY CLOSED the door and started down the street, whistling. For some screwy reason, he felt quite cheerful. He ought to be mad as hell. He wasn't. It was too funny, now. Wilkins! Good Lord—Wilkins! Dineen *and* Wilkins!

It was unfair, though. Definitely unfair. Not that he minded a gal using her wiles to get ahead in a profession; that was a woman's privilege, if she wanted to take advantage of it. But hell's bells—it ought to be against union rules or something for her to be a speed artist at continuity writing on top of it! Either one or the other made the competition tough enough, but both—

It ought to have worried him, but it didn't.

He decided that he must be drunk. And that, again, reminded him of what he was supposed to be doing.

All right, he'd taken the first step. He'd seen Dotty. What had he learned that could be important? What that could have led to murder?

Not Dotty's sex life. Conceivably, someone might have killed Dineen out of jealousy. But not Dotty's uncle, whom she'd never met. Not Frank. Nope, that didn't make sense.

Money, then? The silver inkwell—he'd forgotten about that until Dotty mentioned it. There could be an importance in its being stolen by the killer—if the killer had taken it because it was a gift from Mueller to Dineen.

Under what circumstances had the gift been made? Maybe Mrs. Dineen could tell him that. Maybe she could tell him what other presents, if any—besides the dog collar and the clock— Mueller had given Dineen. Something could be concealed in an inkwell, if the inkwell had been made to conceal it. Or in a clock. Had there been any attempt to steal the clock? And what kind of a clock was it?

He felt a vague excitement, as though he were touching the outer fringes of an answer. What time was it? Too late to go out to Queens this evening to talk to Mrs. Dineen?

Hell, he should have gone out there anyway. Especially since he'd missed the funeral. He could still do it; express condolence, and then ease into the asking of a few questions.

Was he sober enough yet? Well, he would be by the time he got there. It was only eight-thirty by his wrist watch. If he could catch a cab—

One was coming and he flagged it. "Queensborough Bridge,"

he told the driver. "I'll direct you after we cross it; I know how to get there, but not the address."

The cab cut over to Second Avenue and headed north toward the bridge. Tracy noticed that it slowed down once or twice without apparent reason. At Fortieth Street the driver turned east and then north on First Avenue. He turned west on Forty-second, and slowed down again.

He turned around. "There's someone following us," he said. His voice sounded a little scared. "I been making sure before I said anything."

Tracy swore. He'd forgotten Bates' warning about the tailing. Probably he'd been followed all evening—to Barney's and to Dotty's—Well, it didn't matter.

"It's all right," he said. "Let 'em follow."

"Not me, mister," said the cabby. "I don't want no trouble, and I'm not being tailed out to Queens. You get another cab or take the subway or something."

Tracy sighed. "All right," he said. "We're on Forty-second? Take me over to Broadway, then."

On the way he looked back out of the window. Yes, there was the car, a Chevie sedan with two men in the front seat. Big men. Bates hadn't been kidding.

He paid off his cab on the busiest corner in the world. And then, just out of cussedness, he steered an erratic course through the midevening crowd, ducked into the Astor bar and went on through it into the lobby and out another door, and through the crowd again.

When he went down to the subway at the corner, he didn't even bother to look around to see if he was still being followed. One of the men would have had to park the car or stay with it, and if the other hadn't lost him in that jam, then he deserved a subway ride to Queens.

But just the same, out of curiosity, he watched the other people who got on the train. None of them looked like a copper.

And when only two women and an elderly drunk got off at the same stop as Tracy out in Queens, he was sure. He'd lost 'em at the Astor.

He felt pretty sober now, as he walked through the quiet streets toward the Dineen house. He looked at his watch again; it was nine o'clock now; it would be about ten minutes after when he got there. He'd have to apologize and explain that he'd started earlier and had been delayed.

And then he'd head for the nearest restaurant, if they had restaurants out here in Queens. He should have eaten sooner; with the liquor wearing off he was getting hungry as the devil.

Let's see—this was the block. And it would be either the fourth or fifth house from the corner. He didn't remember which and they looked pretty much alike.

He stopped in front of the fourth house, looking from it to the fifth and back again, trying to remember which it was. The time he'd been out here once before had been daytime; things looked different at night.

The fourth house, though, was dark. There were lights on at the fifth. If it was the house in front of which he was standing, then nobody was home unless they'd gone to bed ungodly early.

Might as well try the fifth, the lighted one.

He got as far as the porch steps and saw that he didn't have to go any farther. This, definitely, wasn't the house. The porch and the door were different, and there wasn't any knocker on the door. He remembered admiring the antique brass knocker on the Dineen front door.

Then the other house, the darkened one, was Dineen's, and he'd had his trip for nothing. He retraced his steps to the sidewalk. He looked in again at the Dineen house as he went past the walk leading back to it.

He stopped walking, because there *was* a light there. A dim light at a downstairs window. It looked like it might be a flashlight. He stopped walking and watched.

It *was* a flashlight. It moved, getting dimmer as whoever was holding it moved away from the front of the house. Then brighter, as he came back.

Tracy stood there, wondering what he should do about it.

It could be a burglar. Or it could be one of the family, using a flashlight because a fuse had blown out or something. No, not that. Surely, they'd have spare fuses and the flashlight would be in the cellar where the fuse box would be. Or the persons carrying the flashlight would be heading that way.

The light showed again, briefly, and then vanished.

A thought hit Tracy, hit him hard enough to shake him a bit. If there *was* a burglar in there, it wasn't any ordinary burglar. It would be the killer—the man who had already killed Walther Mueller, Arthur Dineen, and Frank Hrdlicka.

And until now, until this moment, that figure had been an abstraction. Now it wasn't. Killer. A concrete word. *Killer: one who kills.* Not a nice word or a nice thought, alone at night.

Tracy jerked back so he stood in the shadow of a tree between the sidewalk and the curb, and considered what he should do. Go in there?

No, he wasn't crazy, no matter what Bates thought. Without a gun, against a killer who probably had one? Without even a flashlight? Nuts.

There was only one logical, sensible thing to do—go to the lighted house next door and tell them to phone the police. This was a job for the cops, not for Bill Tracy.

He thought, bitterly now, of his cleverness in getting rid of the two policemen who had been following him all evening. He'd give a thousand bucks right now for a sight of that Chevie sedan with two big coppers in it.

He took a last look toward the Dineen house—there wasn't any light at all showing now—and started next door.

Then, suddenly, he knew it was too late to phone for the police. It was too late to do anything, unless it was something foolish. For, in the quiet evening, he heard an unmistakable sound—the opening and closing of the outer door at the back of the house.

The killer was leaving, the back way.

Would he be coming around the house? No, of course not. He'd leave by the alley, if—Yes, there was an alley. Must be, because there was no driveway in past the house, and Tracy remembered that there was a garage at the back.

Probably the killer had left his car—certainly he'd have a car—back there in the alley. If he could get the license number—

Tracy's feet must have been thinking for him, for he was already running to the corner, around the corner, and heading for the mouth of the alley. He ran silently, along the strip of grass between the sidewalk and the curb.

Then the grass ended, but he was running silently anyway, and he remembered that he'd put on crêpe-soled sport shoes when he'd dressing that morning. He stopped in the shadow of a catalpa tree a few yards from the end of the alley, stood there and listened.

There was no sound yet from the alley. Had he been wrong about the car, or about the direction in which the killer would leave? No, there was the soft closing of a car door.

Good; all he had to do was stand there in the shadow. The car would pass him; he could get the number, he hoped. He might even be able to recognize the driver as the car went by.

The hum of a starter, and the low purr of a motor. It was so quiet he could even hear the shift of gears and then the slight change in the motor's sound as the driver let out the clutch. The car was moving now.

But which way? He hadn't thought of that. This end of the alley was nearest to town, nearest to the Queensborough Bridge. But if the car had come out from Manhattan, it was odds on its having *entered* the alley at this end. And—yes the sound of the motor seemed to be receding.

He sprinted to the mouth of the alley and looked in. Yes, there was the dark silhouette of the car against a dim aura of light down at the far end of the alley. It hadn't turned its lights on yet, but it was beginning to move, very slowly, away from him.

He could catch up to it easily, running silently behind it. He could get the rear license number and maybe even recognize the driver, through the back window.

He was halfway down the alley to the car before he saw how wrong he was. Suddenly, then, the headlights of the car flashed on—full upon Tracy, blinding him.

It was coming toward him instead of going away, and the driver stepped on the gas. The gears had changed from low to second; the driver didn't waste time advancing to high. Roaring in second gear, gathering speed, the car came straight at Tracy.

He was running too fast to stop, and there wouldn't be time for him to turn around, anyway, and reach the mouth of the alley. There was only one chance, and Tracy's body rather than his brain thought of it and acted on it.

He turned to run toward the point where, to his left, a low, three-foot fence bridged a three-yard gap between garages. The car turned, too.

Its fender almost scraped his leg as he went over the fence.

Then, lying painfully sprawled on hard-packed ground, just as he had landed, Tracy heard the car slow down momentarily, then shift gears and go on. It reached the street and kept going.

The killer wasn't coming back, then, to accomplish with a gun what his car had so narrowly missed accomplishing. By a margin of inches, Tracy's name was still off the list of victims.

Still dazed by the suddenness with which things had happened, Tracy got to his feet slowly. His knees were shaking, but there didn't seem to be any bones broken.

Well, *that* was what he got for trying to be Dick Tracy instead of Bill. Now there wasn't anything left but to phone the police and tell them what a mess he had made of things, and to take the look of contempt Bates would give him. But nuts to Bates.

He looked out into the alley, looking both ways carefully before he went back over the fence. No one was in sight at either end of the alley. How far would he have to go to find a phone?

Well, he could go to the Dineen house. Why not? The back door was undoubtedly open. That was what he should do, of course. Go there and phone, then wait for the police to come.

He made sure he had the fourth house and then went through

the gate and into the back yard. He reached the steps of the back porch, and hesitated.

What if someone *was* home—asleep upstairs? He shouldn't go barging in without being sure. He went around the house to the front and used the brass knocker. There was a doorbell, too, and he rang it. He could hear it ringing, but there was no answer, no movement anywhere.

The family must be out, then. Unless—

He tried the front door and it was locked. He ran around to the back. Yes, the back door was unlocked. He opened it and stepped into the darkness of what must be the kitchen. There was linoleum underfoot and a faint kitcheny odor.

There was another smell, too. Also a faint one. He couldn't place it until he had his hand on the light switch beside the door and the door was closed behind him. He almost turned and ran out, then. The smell, he knew now, was the smell of blood.

But his fingers flipped the switch. For a second the light blinded him; then he could see.

Rex, the big Doberman pinscher, lay in the middle of the kitchen floor, his head in a pool of blood. One side of his skull had been bashed in by something heavy. This time the killer had finished the job on Rex. Knocked askew and soaked with blood was the bandage that had covered the dog's first wound—the crease from the bullet fired in his master's office last Tuesday.

Tracy took a deep breath and walked around the dog's sprawled body, through a butler's pantry, and into the living room. The phone ought to be around here somewhere. Here were the stairs—

Wait, before he hunted further for the phone, hadn't he better look upstairs, to be sure that the Dineens had really been away from home, and not murdered in their beds? Or perhaps knocked out and tied up? The dog was past help, but what if there were human beings here who weren't? The need for a doctor or an ambulance might be more pressing than the need for the police, and he could get both with one call.

He went on up the stairs, lighting lights as he went, and through the upper part of the house. There were plenty of signs of the burglar—drawers emptied out onto the floor, closets ransacked—but there were no Dineens up there, dead or alive.

Breathing a bit more freely, he went back downstairs and found the phone in a little room off the hallway by the foot of the stairs. He reached for it, then thought that, having searched this far, he might as well look into the one room remaining, before he phoned. Then he could be certain in reporting that there'd been no murder done, except the dog.

The one room he hadn't entered yet was the front room, the one through whose windows he'd seen the flashlight. He went along the hall, reached through the open doorway, and switched on the lights of the front room.

There *had* been murder.

Flat on its back lay the body of a man Tracy didn't know. He was a big man, dressed in a serge suit. He looked like a detective, a police detective. Undoubtedly that was what he was, left here to guard the house. The police must have anticipated the possibility of an attempt at burglary here. They'd thought that a policeman and a police dog, together, would be enough to stop it.

But they'd been wrong; the killer had got both of them, and had made his getaway. He'd almost got himself an extra victim, out there in the alley, while he was getting away.

But those thoughts were going on in the bottom layer, as it were, of Tracy's mind, things to be thought out and sorted out later. On top was sheer and numbing horror.

Not at the fact that murder had been done, but at *how* it had been done.

There was a bullet hole and a red stain on the detective's chest, but it was on the right side, not over the heart. That shot had knocked him down and out. It might have killed him later, as it must have gone through his right lung. But it hadn't killed him instantly.

By the man's face, his eyes, his tongue, there wasn't any doubt about the immediate cause of death—strangulation. And Bill Tracy's eyes were riveted in horror upon the man's neck and necktie.

The tie wasn't around his neck inside the collar; it had been slid up higher than that and used as a garrote, twisted tight by the insertion of a round polished piece of wood—it looked like a rung broken from a chair—in the manner of a tourniquet.

It was no more horrible, in itself, than other methods of murder, except for two facts. First, that it must have been done cold-bloodedly, while the man was unconscious from the bullet wound. And second—

The fact that it made the fourth of Tracy's *Murder Can Be Fun* ideas which had been put to deadly use.

A man strangled with his own cravat.

As Tracy stood there, looking down, he heard footsteps on the sidewalk outside. Footsteps that stopped, then started again, coming closer as though they were turning in the walk back to the house.

They were heavy footsteps, with an official sound to them. It was the heavy tread of a patrolman, a beat cop. Probably he knew that the Dineens were out and that a detective was on guard inside. He'd be wondering why all the lights in the house were on—

The steps reached the porch, sounded on wood.

And panic hit Bill Tracy; hit him hard.

He didn't know why he ran. He knew it was a foolish thing to do. He knew he should wait here, let the policeman in, and explain things, then wait until the homicide men got here. Then explain again and let them question him for the rest of the night.

No, it wasn't a reasonable fear, nor a reasoning one. It was blind panic. It came because the footsteps had come too soon after he'd seen how that necktie had been used. Before he'd had time to assimilate and digest that awful fact.

If they found *him* here now—

That was as far as he could have expressed his fear coherently. But he ran.

As fast as he could run without making a noise. Through the house and out the back door, while the reverberation of the brass knocker on the front door drowned what little sound he may have made.

Across the back yard and into the alley. Through it and across the street and through the next alley. Only then did he stop running, and walk toward the subway station.

Panic walked with him still. The very night seemed to be closing in upon him as he walked, and after he got his breath back it was with difficulty that he kept himself from breaking into a run again.

Luckily, there was no one in the subway station at the moment he walked in. He caught a glimpse of his own face in the mirror of a gum machine. He stopped then, forced himself to stand there long enough to light a cigarette with his shaking hands, and to compose his features before he went down to the tracks.

It seemed hours before a train came.

There was an atmosphere of unreality about that ride back to Manhattan. There were other people in the car, but they seemed more like ghosts than real fellow-passengers. Even the little old lady who sat directly across from him and smiled at him benignantly, didn't seem quite real.

It was a nightmare ride. He tried not to think, but that was worse—because he *felt* instead.

He didn't recover the semblance of calmness until he reached his own flat at the Smith Arms.

He mixed himself a drink, and found it tasted terrible. And his hands were still shaky. He put them into his pockets and sat in the Morris chair. He looked at the door and wondered if he'd locked it. He thought he had, but he got up and made certain, and then went back to the chair again. His hands were trembling a little less.

He remembered that he was hungry, and then decided that he wasn't. Then he decided maybe he was. Anyway, going out for coffee and a sandwich would be something to do. He couldn't think of anything *else* to do. For once, definitely, he didn't want a drink.

At Thompson's, he had coffee and two sandwiches.

He wondered, was Millie by any chance home and awake? He wanted to talk to someone. On the way back he looked up at her window; it was dark.

Dick? No, he didn't want to talk to anyone after all, unless it was Millie.

He thought, if I end up killed or in jail, it'll be her fault. Hers and Lee Randolph's. Damn 'em both for talking me into making a fool of myself.

He went back to his room and sat down in the Morris chair again, trying to think.

Outside, a clock struck midnight.

And that meant it wasn't Sunday any more; it was the end of his first day of vacation, his first day of marvelous freedom.

Was he going to sit there and jitter all night? Why the hell didn't he just go to bed, if he couldn't think of anything better to do?

He got up and took off his necktie and opened his collar. He was reaching for the tie rack when the idea hit him.

Suddenly, just like that, he knew the main part of the answer. He knew who the killer was. There was only one person who could be the killer.

CHAPTER 14

HE ALMOST dropped the tie. He said "My God!" and stared at himself in the mirror. It was utterly incredible. But there it was.

It had to be true because there wasn't any other answer. It was like a chess problem. There was only one key move, and when you made it, everything fell into place and you saw the reason for each piece being placed just so.

It had been perfect, almost. Except for the necktie. That's where the slip-up had been. The killer hadn't realized one little thing.

Slowly Tracy's hand came back with the tie he'd been about

to hang up, and he put it back on. He adjusted the knot very carefully, and then went back to the closet to get his coat.

He put it on and then stopped to think again. He'd been going out to look up Bates, but he couldn't—yet. He wasn't, come to think of it, one hundred per cent sure. Just ninety-nine and forty-four one-hundredths. There *might* be some other explanation. He didn't see how, but there might be. He thought a minute, and knew how he could find out.

The thought scared him, but there it was.

Was he crazy enough to stick his neck out again, a second time in one evening? If he only had a gun—

Before he could change his mind, he picked up the phone. He gave the number of Dick Kreburn's hotel, and then Dick's room number.

After a minute, Dick's voice—with only a trace of hoarseness now—came to him.

"This is Tracy," he said. "Listen, have you still got that pistol—that automatic, you had a couple of months ago?"

"Sure, Tracy. Want to shoot somebody?"

"N-no, not exactly. But I *am* in a jam, Dick. Could I borrow it for a few days, just to carry?"

"Why, I guess so, Tracy. I haven't any holster for it. But it's a thirty-two; you *can* carry it in your pocket if you have to."

"That's okay. You home for the night? Going to be up long enough for me to get it?"

"I was just leaving, Tracy. Just luck you caught me at all. I was in a poker game uptown and they cleaned me out of the cash I had with me—it wasn't a fortune—and I came back to my room to pick up some money I had here, and I'm going back. But your place is on my way. Shall I drop the gun off with you?"

"That'll be swell. How soon will you be here?"

"Might be almost an hour. I got a couple of other things to do. And there's no hurry about getting back to the game; it's good for all night, if not longer."

"Okay, Dick. Be seeing you."

He put the receiver back, and started to pace up and down the room. Nearly an hour. Hell.

He thought about a drink, and decided again that he didn't want one. A cup of coffee, though—

Why not? It would kill time for that hour. He went down to Thompson's, leaving his light on and his door an inch ajar so Dick would go on in if he got there early. He had two cups of coffee, with his eye on the clock, and that killed three-quarters of an hour, so he went back to the apartment building, and upstairs.

Dick wasn't there yet.

He was getting definitely scared now. He sat down in the Morris chair, and went over everything again very carefully in his mind. He must be right; it fitted too well to be wrong. It *had* to be—

There was a soft tap at the door and he said, "Come in," and Dick Kreburn came in and said, "Hi, Tracy. Here it is."

"Thanks, Dick."

Tracy took the gun and looked it over. He pulled out the clip and saw it was loaded, jacked open the chamber and saw it wasn't. He put the clip back in and worked the slide again so one of the steel-jacketed bullets went up into the firing chamber. He snicked off the safety catch. Dick Kreburn was watching him. He said, "Looks like you know how to handle one."

"Yeah," Tracy said, "I do. Put up your hands, Dick."

Kreburn's face went blank. He took a slow step backward and raised his hands slowly. He said, "Tracy, if you're not kidding, that was a hell of a dirty trick."

Tracy said, "I'm not kidding. And it's not as dirty a trick as four murders."

"You're crazy."

"Back up and sit down in that Morris chair, Dick. And you can put your hands down when you get there, if you keep them on the arms of the chair."

"Damn you, Tracy—"

"Sit down. I'm giving you a break. You think this was a dirty trick, but it's not as dirty as calling the police and putting them on you without listening to you first. I'm going to tell you how

I figure what happened, and then if you can show me I'm wrong, I won't call them. What have you got to lose?"

Kreburn laughed, without amusement. He said, "My life, if you're not careful. That's a touchy trigger and your knuckle looks white against it. All right, I'll listen. What's this about four murders? Last I heard, it was two you were worried about."

Tracy backed to the desk and sat down on it. He relaxed his finger a trifle on the trigger, but kept the gun aimed at Dick as he rested it on his knee.

He said, "Walther Mueller was the first. You followed him from the plane to his hotel and went to his room to rob him. From what I've heard and read about it, you probably didn't intend to kill him—you slugged him to keep him quiet, but he had a soft skull and he died."

"Why would I have—?"

"Just listen, first. The killer in this case—and that's you—can be only one thing. A professional jewel thief. You weren't after the pearls he brought; you would have known they'd be held in the customs. You must have had a tip, from South America, that he was smuggling in something a hell of a lot more valuable than those pearls.

"That's easy to figure. A man no older than he wouldn't attempt to retire for life on the small amount those pearls and his bank draft came to. He had something else—maybe diamonds —that he wanted to bring in without paying duty on them. Something that *would* bring him enough to retire on.

"But you didn't find the diamonds—let's call them that. He didn't have them with him."

"Didn't he?"

"No. So you watched what happened. You may have attended the inquest; maybe you found out things in other ways; I don't know. But you knew those diamonds had to be somewhere, so you kept close track.

"You learned about Dineen. You learned he'd sent the Dineens presents. You got the hunch that he'd sent the diamonds to Dineen, probably without Dineen's knowledge, concealed in—

well, in an inkwell or something. But you didn't know just what presents he'd sent. You'd have to get close to Dineen to find out.

"And that's where you first roped me in. Until two months ago, we'd met once or twice in bars; I didn't even know your name. But you knew mine and where I worked, and you got chummy. I was a sucker; I took your word that you were an actor who needed a job and I wrote you into the scripts, introduced you to Dineen, and got you a job working right under him. So you got to know him and got to know about the inkwell and where it came from. And you saw it was big and ornate enough to conceal anything short of a bunch of bananas. And maybe you thought it was the only thing Mueller had sent Dineen.

"And to get it, you swiped one of my script ideas on how to—"

"Tracy, you *are* crazy. What you've said so far makes sense except for the pronoun you're using. But according to your own story, nobody could have read that script of yours."

"Nobody but someone Frank Hrdlicka knew as a friend of mine. There's only one way it could have happened, Dick. Monday evening I left that Santa script in my machine and went out. You came here looking for me, and saw Frank, and he used his passkey to let you come in to wait for me in the apartment. He knew I wouldn't mind."

Tracy's voice was getting surer now. He went on: "You read that script, and the others. You saw in that script an idea how you could hold up Dineen and get the inkwell, and never be recognized. Maybe the idea tickled your sense of humor. Dammit, it *was* a good idea.

"And you thought once you got the inkwell you'd have the diamonds and do a fadeout, so the thing would be over. But the idea went wrong; the dog was there, and you had to shoot, and killed Dineen. And when you got the inkwell home, there was nothing hidden in it.

"So you couldn't fade out of the picture yet; you wanted to stay Dick Kreburn—instead of whatever your real name is—

and keep in touch with things until you found out where the stuff really was.

"And so you came back here and killed Frank—*because Frank could have told that you had access to those scripts.* In fact, I'd already decided to ask Frank whether anybody had been in here Monday evening.

"And—either because of a macabre sense of humor or to make things as complicated as you could—you remembered one of my scripts had been about a janitor, and you followed that script in killing Frank."

Dick Kreburn was leaning forward in the chair now, interest and nothing else showing in his face. He said, "You're making a good story, Tracy. Except, like I said, for the pronoun. And did you mention four murders?"

"You know about that. Tonight. You'd learned about the clock and maybe about other presents the Dineens had received, and you went out there to collect them. You killed the detective on guard out there, and you killed Rex. You followed another *Murder Can Be Fun* idea on the policeman. Too bad I never wrote a script about a man being run down in an alley by an auto—but you missed getting me, anyway."

"That all?" Kreburn asked. He leaned back in the chair again. "It's good, Tracy. I really think maybe you've got something, except why pick on *me?*"

"Two reasons—besides the fact that I first met you at just about the right time, and you talked me into getting you the job at KRBY. One of them is the laryngitis you had. Or the sore throat. You got that from wearing a heavy flannel Santa Claus suit over your regular clothes on a sweltering August day. You were probably soaked with sweat before you got rid of it."

Dick Kreburn chuckled. "You call *that* proof?"

"No," Tracy said. "But the other reason is the important one. It's this. There never was a *Murder Can Be Fun* script about a man being strangled with his own necktie. The furthest that ever got was a rough note in the notebook I carry in my pocket. *Nobody* knew about it. Not even Millie Wheeler. Not even Inspector Bates. And I tore up the page and threw it away.

"But I remembered tonight that when I took you home in a taxi from the radio station, and wouldn't let you talk to me because of your throat, I passed you that notebook to write out whatever you wanted to say. You leafed through it to find a blank page. That's when you could have—and must have—seen that notation about a man being strangled with his own cravat—and you're the only person besides myself who ever handled that notebook."

Kreburn chuckled again. He said, "Pretty good, Tracy. Pretty good."

Tracy stood up, keeping the gun pointed carefully, keeping his distance.

He said, "And now, can you tell me any reason why I shouldn't phone the cops?"

"Yes," Kreburn said, "When you phoned me to ask for a gun, I thought you might have got smart and decided to pull a fast one like this, Tracy. I wanted to hear what you had to say. I knew you'd be smart enough to look over the gun to be sure it was loaded—but I didn't think you'd go so far as to check whether or not the firing pin had been taken out."

Another pistol—one with a long silencer on the barrel—was coming out from under Kreburn's coat as he stood up.

Tracy's finger tightened on the trigger of the automatic in his hand—because there could be such a thing as a bluff—and the spring of the automatic clicked metallically. That was all; there wasn't any shot.

Something in Tracy's mind said to him, "Here it comes—" but there wasn't any numbness in his mind.

Even as the silenced gun was centering on Tracy's chest, he saw the door that led to the other room of his apartment, the bedroom, opening slowly and silently.

He jerked his eyes back to Kreburn's face and said, "Wait, Dick," because, if help was coming, even a fraction of a second's delay might save him.

Over Dick's shoulder, he could see now who was opening the

door. Two heads showed in the opening doorway—Bates and Corey, Corey's head towering over that of the smaller man.

Only if they didn't shoot, and Kreburn did—?

He said, "Wait, Dick. You haven't got the diamonds yet. And I know where they are."

Kreburn's face didn't register belief, but his finger stopped tightening on the trigger. He said, "You're stalling, Tracy."

"What good does it do me to stall? Stall, hell; I want a bargain. I want to get out of this alive if I tell you where the diamonds are."

The door was wide open now, and Bates was tiptoeing through it; he made no sound.

Kreburn asked, "Where are they?"

"If I tell you," Tracy said, "you'll shoot. We'll have to work out something better than that."

"Tell me, and I'll tie you up and leave you. You'll be found some time tomorrow."

Bates was coming alongside Kreburn now, walking silently as a cat. There was a pistol in his hand and it was lifting, not to shoot, but to crack down across Kreburn's hand that gripped the silenced gun. Corey was standing still back in the doorway. There was a gun in his hand, too; a forty-five automatic that looked as big as a cannon.

Tracy said, "Fair enough. But how can I take your word that you'll—?"

That was as far as he had to go. Bates struck. Kreburn yelped, half from pain and half from surprise, and the silenced gun thudded against the carpet. Kreburn turned on Bates, and then Corey was there—seeming to have covered the distance between the doorway and the killer in nothing flat—with the big forty-five jammed into Kreburn's side.

Tracy sat back down on the desk. Not because he had decided to, but because his knees had decided not to hold him up any longer.

He fumbled a cigarette out of his case and got it to his mouth. He tried to light it, and Bates watched him and grinned. After

177

a few seconds, Bates stepped forward, struck a match, and held it for him.

Tracy asked, "H-how did you happen to be in there?"

Bates said, "In a minute." He picked up the phone and said, "Get the wagon, George. Then you can go home."

He put down the receiver. He grinned at Tracy again, and sat down on the arm of the Morris chair. He said, "There's been a bug on your phone line for three days. Man on duty in the basement—it's George right now—in the back room of what used to be Frank's quarters.

"When we came around to arrest you half an hour ago, we dropped in on George to see what had been going on—and we learned you'd asked Kreburn to come over and bring a rod. And you'd just been checked into Thompson's, so we thought we'd come in and wait to see what you wanted with Kreburn and the rod before we made the pinch."

Tracy said, "You took a hell of a chance with my life, waiting that long. Next time, arrest me."

Bates laughed. "He might have shot you, sure. Then again, you might have shot him. Call it a horse apiece."

"I could call it worse," Tracy said. "You were going to arrest me?"

"Hell, yes. You left a trail a mile wide out to Queens. Those men you ducked had the license number of the cab they'd been trailing. When they lost you at Forty-second and Broadway, they checked on the cab and found out where its stand was. Then they found from the cabby you'd been heading for Queens.

"And then—well, we got the report from Queens. Blame us for coming to get you? And—say!"

"Say what?"

"Were you kidding, or do you know where the diamonds are? If there are any, that is."

"I'd like to guess. I'll bet Kreburn never happened to learn that the dog collar was a present, and a pretty recent one, from Mueller. That collar's got twelve or fifteen pretty large studs, each one big enough to hold a ten- or twenty-carat stone inside it. And if there *are* any diamonds, I *hope* that's where they are —because my dear friend here had two perfectly good chances to take that collar, and didn't. That's why I'm pretty sure he didn't know the collar came from Mueller."

Bates nodded slowly.

He said, "There's red tape. There's a lot of paper work to washing up four murders. We need statements and stuff. Want to come down and get it over with, or sleep?"

"Sleep?" Tracy asked. "What's sleep?"

Then he remembered. "Go ahead, Inspector," he said, "I got a call to make. If I'm not downstairs in time for a ride in the wagon, I'll follow in a cab."

Bates nodded. He and Corey took Kreburn out.

Tracy called Lee Randolph at the *Blade*. He said, "Here's our story, Lee." And then he talked fast for ten minutes straight. He added, "If I find the hunch about the dog collar is right, I'll call you back. Save that for a lead for the final."

"Swell, Tracy; listen, I'm sorry I—"

"Skip it. See you tomorrow."

He hung up before Lee could say any more.

When he got downstairs, the wagon had come and gone. That was all right with Tracy. He went to headquarters by way of Barney's, and had a few beers with the late shift from the *Blade*. He played the *Beer Barrel Polka* twice on the juke box.

From Barney's he would have gone straight to headquarters except that he remembered to stop by Stan Hrdlicka's place to tell him about it, and by that time he'd forgotten how the slivovitz had bitten him once. It bit him again.

But not so badly this time; he woke up in Stan's bed, of his own volition and bright and early at eight o'clock in the morning.

He felt swell. He bought a clean shirt, took a Turkish bath, got shaved at a barber shop, and felt marvelous.

He got to Bates' office by ten, and got away by eleven. He had a momentary twinge of conscience when he learned that the stones—they'd been matched diamonds—*had* been in the studs of the dog collar. He felt better when he found a final of the

Blade still left on a newsstand and saw that Lee had got it in time anyway.

He had breakfast, and then went to KRBY. He breezed into Wilkins' office, whistling.

He saw a copy of the *Blade* on Wilkins' desk. Wilkins glanced at Tracy, back at the paper, and then at Tracy again. He said, "Good morning, Mr. Tracy." His voice was friendly. "I see you have solved your difficulties."

"Yes," said Tracy. "Have you?"

Wilkins stiffened a little. He said, "I hope that now that your mind is free from—ah—the worries to which it has undoubtedly been subjected, you will feel up to writing again. But—ah—would you care to try your hand at something different? Miss Mueller appears to be doing so well—"

"Doesn't she?" said Tracy.

Wilkins frowned. He said, "If you will read your contra Mr. Tracy, you will discover that we are empowered to use y as we see fit, provided only that we meet the financial ter Your contract does not specify that you must write *Mill Millions.*"

"And how, Mr. Wilkins," asked Tracy, "do you see fit to use me?"

"We would like you to try your hand at writing commercials, Mr. Tracy."

Tracy grinned. "And if I refuse, the contract terminates?"

"Ah—yes."

Tracy stood up. "I shall not belabor the obvious by telling you what to do with the contract, Mr. Wilkins. Pleace give Miss Mueller my regards. And my pay check."

He left, even more cheerful than he had come.

He went to see Lee Randolph at Lee's hotel, waking him up out of a sound sleep.

He went back to Barney's, had a beer and a sandwich, and played the *Beer Barrel Polka* on the juke box.

Then, from Barney's booth, he phoned Millie Wheeler.

"Tracy!" she said. "I just read the morning papers. I'm so glad. I knew you could do it!"

"Uh-huh," said Tracy modestly. "I'm wonderful. I've got even better news. I'm bounced at the studio. I'm back to being a reporter, at about half my erstwhile income. Think we could live on that?"

"Huh? You mean—?"

"I mean I think maybe I love you. I think maybe I've been an awful sap for a long time. I think maybe you should quit working and I should quit drinking—except for beers with the boys at Barney's—say, isn't that lovely alliteration?—beers with the boys at Barney's—and maybe we should forget how smart we are and raise a kid or two and play bridge in the suburbs. Will you meet me at the city hall?"

Millie took a deep breath. She asked, "When?"

"Half an hour?"

"Give me two hours, you big lug. I'll skip buying a trousseau, but Tracy, a bride's got to take a bath and put on clean underwear."

"An hour and a half," said Tracy. "Meet you there at a quarter of three. 'Bye now."

He came out of the phone booth and went over to the bar whistling the *Beer Barrel Polka*. He said, "A short beer, Barney."

Barney drew it and scooped off the foam. Then he went around the bar and put a nickel in the juke box. It started playing the *Beer Barrel Polka,* and he went back behind the bar and said, "That damn tune."

He drew himself a beer. "You say you're starting in again at the *Blade* tomorrow night?"

"Right," said Tracy.

"There'll be a pinochle game about eleven this evening when the boys come in. Drop around."

"I'll try," said Tracy. "Might be a little hard to get away this evening, but I'll try."

ct,
ou
ns.
lie's

FINE MYSTERY AND SUSPENSE
TITLES FROM CARROLL & GRAF

- [ ] Bentley, E.C./TRENT'S OWN CASE $3.95
- [ ] Blake, Nicholas/MURDER WITH MALICE $3.95
- [ ] Blake, Nicholas/A TANGLED WEB $3.50
- [ ] Boucher, Anthony/THE CASE OF THE BAKER STREET IRREGULARS $3.95
- [ ] Boucher, Anthony (ed.)/FOUR AND TWENTY BLOODHOUNDS $3.95
- [ ] Brand, Christianna/DEATH IN HIGH HEELS $3.95
- [ ] Brand, Christianna/FOG OF DOUBT $3.50
- [ ] Brand, Christianna/TOUR DE FORCE $3.95
- [ ] Brown, Fredric/THE LENIENT BEAST $3.50
- [ ] Brown, Fredric/MURDER CAN BE FUN $3.95
- [ ] Brown, Fredric/THE SCREAMING MIMI $3.50
- [ ] Browne, Howard/THIN AIR $3.50
- [ ] Buchan, John/JOHN MACNAB $3.95
- [ ] Buchan, John/WITCH WOOD $3.95
- [ ] Burnett, W.R./LITTLE CAESAR $3.50
- [ ] Butler, Gerald/KISS THE BLOOD OFF MY HANDS $3.95
- [ ] Carr, John Dickson/THE BRIDE OF NEWGATE $3.95
- [ ] Carr, John Dickson/CAPTAIN CUT-THROAT $3.95
- [ ] Carr, John Dickson/DARK OF THE MOON $3.50
- [ ] Carr, John Dickson/DEADLY HALL $3.95
- [ ] Carr, John Dickson/DEMONIACS $3.95
- [ ] Carr, John Dickson/THE DEVIL IN VELVET $3.95
- [ ] Carr, John Dickson/THE EMPEROR'S SNUFF-BOX $3.50
- [ ] Carr, John Dickson/FIRE, BURN! $3.50
- [ ] Carr, John Dickson/IN SPITE OF THUNDER $3.50
- [ ] Carr, John Dickson/LOST GALLOWS $3.50
- [ ] Carr, John Dickson/MOST SECRET $3.95
- [ ] Carr, John Dickson/NINE WRONG ANSWERS $3.50
- [ ] Carr, John Dickson/PAPA LA-BAS $3.95

- [ ] Hughes, Dorothy B./THE FALLEN SPARROW $3.50
- [ ] Hughes, Dorothy B./IN A LONELY PLACE $3.50
- [ ] Hughes, Dorothy B./RIDE THE PINK HORSE $3.95
- [ ] Innes, Hammond/ATLANTIC FURY $3.50
- [ ] Innes, Hammond/THE LAND GOD GAVE TO CAIN $3.50
- [ ] Kitchin, C. H. B./DEATH OF HIS UNCLE $3.95
- [ ] Kitchin, C. H. B./DEATH OF MY AUNT $3.50
- [ ] L'Amour, Louis/THE HILLS OF HOMICIDE $2.95
- [ ] Lewis, Norman/THE MAN IN THE MIDDLE $3.50
- [ ] MacDonald, John D./TWO $2.50
- [ ] MacDonald, Philip/THE RASP $3.50
- [ ] Mason, A.E.W./AT THE VILLA ROSE $3.50
- [ ] Mason, A.E.W./THE HOUSE OF THE ARROW $3.50
- [ ] Priestley, J.B./SALT IS LEAVING $3.95
- [ ] Queen, Ellery/THE FINISHING STROKE $3.95
- [ ] Rogers, Joel T./THE RED RIGHT HAND $3.50
- [ ] 'Sapper'/BULLDOG DRUMMOND $3.50
- [ ] Siodmak, Curt/DONOVAN'S BRAIN $3.50
- [ ] Symons, Julian/BLAND BEGINNING $3.95
- [ ] Symons, Julian/BOGUE'S FORTUNE $3.95
- [ ] Symons, Julian/THE BROKEN PENNY $3.95
- [ ] Wainwright, John/ALL ON A SUMMER'S DAY $3.50
- [ ] Wallace, Edgar/THE FOUR JUST MEN $2.95
- [ ] Waugh, Hillary/SLEEP LONG, MY LOVE $3.95
- [ ] Willeford, Charles/THE WOMAN CHASER $3.95

Available from fine bookstores everywhere or use this coupon for ordering.